"Where have you guys been? It's not a good idea to be late when you're running for public office."

Chris pulled Stretch aside and let J.R. continue to the dugout. "I fixed it so there would be a lot of kids here for you to impress today. The school photographer may even show up, so next time you're going to be late, let me know."

"You sound like my mother. We were practicing at my house," Stretch said.

"I thought you might sign autographs after the game. Maybe you can make a speech, nothing fancy, just casual and cool."

"You want me to make all the outs, too, I suppose."

"Well, it wouldn't hurt, especially since I told them you'd make a home run, preferably a grand slam."

Stretch's mouth dropped open. "What? I can't guarantee that."

"Ah, it's no sweat for you."

Stretch grabbed Chris's arm. "Stop making promises that I can't keep."

THE HIGH-FIVES™

GRAND SLAM

S. S. Gorman

A MINSTREL® BOOK

PUBLISHED BY POCKET BOOKS

New York   London   Toronto   Sydney   Tokyo   Singapore

This book is a work of fiction. Names, characters, places, and incidents are either the product of the author's imagination or are used fictitiously. Any resemblance to actual events or locales or persons, living or dead, is entirely coincidental.

A MINSTREL PAPERBACK *ORIGINAL*

A Minstrel Book published by
POCKET BOOKS, a division of Simon & Schuster Inc.
1230 Avenue of the Americas, New York, NY 10020

ISBN: 0-671-74502-6

First Minstrel Books printing March 1992

10 9 8 7 6 5 4 3 2 1

A MINSTREL BOOK and colophon are registered trademarks
of Simon & Schuster Inc.

Printed in the U.S.A.

With love to Maryl,
Ashley, and Bradley,
true Grand Slammers

Chapter 1

THE CARD

"Okay, this is my final offer," tall, lanky Stretch Evans said as he rested his elbows on his knees. The twelve-year-old Afro-American held a thick stack of baseball cards in one hand. "I'll trade you the Yankee of your choice, my Ozzie Smith All-Star, and"—he slipped a card from the bottom of pile—"my Bo Jackson rookie card, all for your Mickey Mantle 1958."

"Don't trade your Bo Jackson," Stretch's friend, eleven-year-old J. R. Klipp, said with a gasp. "That's one of your best cards."

"Keep quiet," Stretch blurted out, his dark brown eyes darting back to J.R. "What do you say, Hank?"

Hank Thompson was a chubby seventh grader who hung out with a group of kids who called themselves the Raiders. Hank's father had given him the valuable base-ball card, and Hank'd been taunting Stretch with it for weeks. "I don't think so," Hank answered with a shrug.

"Come on, Thompson, you know it's a good trade."

"Too good," the brown-eyed, freckle-faced Klipp replied.

Stretch wasn't ready to give up. He held the Bo Jackson close to Hank's face. "You know you want it."

Hank sat quietly for a moment. "Maybe, but not just yet."

"Well, when then?" Stretch added without missing a beat.

Hank sighed. "Look, this Mickey Mantle is a very rare card."

"And so is the Jackson," Stretch fired back. "Even the Beckett says it's going to be one of the most highly coveted cards of the decade. And the Beckett is practically the bible of baseball cards."

"Then why do you want to trade it?" J.R. asked.

"I don't," Stretch said, frustrated with his friend. He wished J.R. would leave him alone. "It's just that I want the Mantle more," he said under his breath.

"I'm not ready," Hank said, standing up. "Not today."

Stretch stood, too, and his long arms pushed out of the cuffs of his Colorado Buffaloes sweatshirt. "Come on, man, I thought you really wanted to trade."

"I changed my mind. But I'll think about it." He grabbed his Dugan Junior High baseball cap, slapped it on his head, and ran up the stairs that led from the dugout to the playing field.

"Well, don't wait too long, the offer ends today." Stretch went up the steps and walked to the chain link fence that cut off the baseball diamond from the bleachers. "That guy's driving me crazy. Every day he says he's ready to trade and then at the last minute he backs out."

J.R. shoved his small hands deep into his jeans pockets. "Maybe it's because he knows you want it so bad."

"Yeah, maybe. I really thought I had him this time."

"Me, too, but I'm glad you didn't give up your Bo Jackson. That's one of your best cards."

"Yeah, it would be a drag to waste it on Thompson." Stretch ran his fingers through his short Afro haircut. "I really want that Mantle though."

"Maybe next time."

Stretch couldn't hide his disappointment. "Yeah, maybe. It would make my collection complete if I could get my hands on that card," he added almost to himself.

J.R. nodded and his straight dark brown hair flopped in his eyes. "Any sixth grader in my class at Bressler would kill to have your collection the way it is now."

"Yeah, well, it may be good, but Thompson is the only seventh grader at Dugan who has a '58 Mantle."

"You'll get it. He was really close to dealing today, don't you think?"

"Yep, but close isn't good enough. You know that old saying. Close is only good enough in horseshoes and hand grenades." Stretch snap-popped his fingers.

"Come on, we'd better get going if we want to meet the rest of the gang over at Mike's Diner. We're already late for our High-Fives meeting."

Stretch put his cards in a special plastic case and then

slid them into the small pocket of his red backpack. "Yeah, let's go. Gadget will be writing our names in the tardy column of the High-Fives blue spiral."

J.R. smiled. "I can see his glasses fogging up from the steam."

Stretch flung his blue Cubs jacket over his shoulder. It was an unusually warm spring day in Conrad, Colorado. The buds were starting to show on the trees, and in a few weeks the lilac bushes around the university would be in full bloom. Easter break would be over the next day. The final quarter would begin—and so would spring baseball. "Yep, Chris will have checked his watch three times by now."

"And my brother will be ordering his cheeseburger and onion rings," J.R. said, running ahead of Stretch.

"And don't forget his tall glass of water." Stretch chuckled to himself as the duo picked up their pace and headed across the park toward their favorite hangout, Mike's Diner. "I guess we know each other pretty well, huh? Chris will order grilled cheese, fries, and—"

"A strawberry malt," the part Sioux boy interrupted. "And don't forget Gadget's brain food." Both announced his order together in a singsong manner. "A tuna platter on rye, a cup of minestrone soup, and an orange soda pop." They laughed and exchanged high-fives.

"You're right, we know each other pretty well," Stretch added.

"This will be our second baseball season together. We should have a pretty hot team."

"Best in the league," Stretch said matter-of-factly.

"You'll probably be the MVP for the zillionth time in a row. You want to play left field again?"

"You bet, but I learned my lesson last year. I'll play where the coach wants me to. Besides, I'd kind of like to give shortstop a try."

"Really?" J.R. said, surprised. Stretch was an outstanding baseball player and was known for his great fielding and consistently high batting average.

"Hey, why not."

J.R. squinted into the midmorning sun. "I'd like to try first or third base, but I bet I'll end up as catcher, especially if Alex pitches again."

"She's good, there's no doubt about it. Who'd ever think a tall, skinny girl could have such an arm." Stretch slapped the bark on a large cottonwood tree. "Your brother's going to play, isn't he?"

"Oh, sure. He complains a lot, but deep down he's dying to get back on the field. I caught him practicing a few swings in front of the bathroom mirror the other day."

"That's our Jack, feisty on the outside, marshmallow inside." The boys stopped in front of a small clapboard building with a dark green door and a sign hanging overhead that read, Mike's Diner in yellow letters. "Did Jack get straight A's again last report card?"

J.R. grasped the wrought-iron railing and pulled himself up two stairs at a time. "Yep, but don't tell him I told you."

"Amazing, I work my tail off to get B's, and your

brother does his best to keep his grades a secret. If I got straight A's I'd be shouting my lungs out."

"He doesn't think it's cool." J.R. stopped before opening the door. "Kids have been making fun of him for years. He's too short, he's part Sioux, our folks are divorced, and he has a bad temper. You wouldn't believe the kids that come up to me to pick a fight. I wish they'd remember he's the one with the wavy hair, and I'm the one with the freckles."

"You have to admit you guys look a lot alike."

J.R. put his hands up to his ears. "Don't say that when Jack is around."

"Don't worry, I may not get straight A's, but I've hung out with the High-Fives long enough not to be stupid."

Chapter 2

ROLL CALL

Stretch opened the heavy door to Mike's Diner, and he and J.R. stepped into the dimly lit restaurant, blinking to adjust to the darkness. "What'd I tell ya," Stretch said after a minute, "the gang's all here."

"Hey, where've you guys been? You're late," blond, blue-eyed Chris Morton said, pointing to his watch.

Stretch and J.R. walked closer to the gangs' usual booth tucked in the back corner of the diner. "I told you he'd be looking at his watch," Stretch said.

A boy with sandy-colored hair and hazel eyes pushed up his wire-rimmed glasses. "I was about to mark you tardy in the notebook," Gadget teased and waved the High-Fives' blue spiral notebook in the air.

"Excuse us, Mr. William Irving Shaw," Stretch joked back. "I thought this was a club, Gadget, not history class."

Gadget grinned. "I guess I take my job as secretary too seriously sometimes."

"That's one of the reasons we like you, Gadget," J.R. said as he slid into the booth next to his brainy friend. "Besides, we were up to some pretty serious business ourselves. Right, Stretch?"

"You got it, kiddo." Stretch sat on the opposite side next to Chris.

"Don't tell me," Jack Klipp, J.R.'s older brother by fourteen months, said, putting his elbows on the table-top. "You were trying to trade for Thompson's Mantle again?"

"How'd you guess?" J.R. asked.

"Because it's what Stretch's been doing for the past three weeks," Jack answered.

"Did you get it?" Chris asked eagerly.

Stretch shrugged. "Close, but no cigar."

"Ah, man, he's got you now. He knows you're desperate," Chris added.

J.R. made triangles with the silverware at his place. "Possessed is more like it."

"Hey, some things are worth fighting for," Stretch added, defending himself.

"I hear there's going to be a raffle at the Swap Shop this Saturday," Gadget said. "Maybe he's got a Mantle."

Stretch perked up. "Really?"

"Yeah, Max said he's going to give away three vintage cards, and a couple other prizes. Whenever you buy anything at his store this week, a duplicate of your receipt will go into a bin, and then next Saturday at one o'clock they'll have a drawing. You could win something pretty cool."

"Maybe now is the time for me to buy the George Brett I've been looking at," Stretch said. "My dad said he'd get it for my birthday, but that's not for another two months."

"I might get that Topps American Division special issue series," J.R. said.

Jack stared at his brother in disbelief. "The whole series?"

"Okay, maybe just a couple of cards," J.R. murmured.

Gadget tapped his fork on the tabletop. "Excuse me, guys. I like trading cards as much as the next kid, but we have baseball practice in an hour, and we should get on with our meeting."

"Gadget's right," Chris said. "I officially call the High-Fives weekly meeting to order. Should we dispense with the minutes of the last meeting?"

"Hold on," Gadget said sharply. "We always dispense with the minutes. I don't see any reason for me to take them if I'm not ever going to read them."

"Okay, Gadg, right after roll call we'll read the minutes of the last meeting," Stretch said, rolling his eyes.

"Roll call," Chris repeated. The gang raised their right hands and made a group high-five in the center of the table. "Thumbs-up."

Jack ran his thumb along the palms of the other guys' hands. "Yep."

"Index," Chris said quietly. Gadget, whose secret

club name corresponded to the fact that he was as intelligent as a walking index file, full of information and facts, answered "Present."

"Center." Chris nodded to Stretch.

"Yo," Stretch, the tallest member, answered as he ran his finger across the other hands.

"Ringo, the ringleader, is here," Chris said, tapping the palms of each hand. "And Pinky, the pinkster, alias P.K."

J.R., the youngest and smallest member, went through the same motions with his little finger and answered "Here."

Each boy thumped his fingers on the tabletop, high-fived the kid sitting next to him and then wiggled his fingers. "This meeting is officially called to order."

"I've been thinking," Stretch jumped in before anyone spoke. "If Max is going to have a raffle, why couldn't we have one, too?"

"How's that?" J.R. quizzed.

"Well, we all have lots of different cards—duplicates and others that don't fit into our collections, right?"

"A drawerful," Jack grumbled.

"Well, why not trade and sell some of our cards?"

"How about before the game on Friday?" Gadget suggested.

"I don't know," Chris grumbled. "That's our first game—shouldn't we be concentrating on playing? It's going to be different this year, since we're in the city league now."

"Then how about after?" Stretch quickly added.

"Lots of kids will be there, and since we'll just have won, we'll be ready to celebrate. We could even do it here."

"I'm willing to try," J.R. said.

"Okay, if there aren't any objections," Chris began, "we'll set up our own traders convention after the game on Friday. All in favor, say aye."

"Aye," the gang said together.

"All opposed," Chris continued. It was silent. "Great. Maybe if it goes well, we can have one after each victory."

"Wow, this is super." Stretch grinned. "It doesn't get better than this. Baseball game first, trading second."

"Just make sure you keep your priorities in that order." Jack sneered at Stretch.

"Don't worry about me," Stretch fired back. "I've been hitting well in practice. I'll be equally hot in a game. The trading session will give me added incentive."

Chris glanced around the table. "All right then, is there any other new business?"

"Or new orders?" Alex Tye, Mike's daughter and the team's pitcher, interrupted as she approached the table.

"How many times do we have to tell you to stop sneaking up on us," Jack said.

Gadget slammed the secret blue spiral closed. "Hi, Alex."

Alex flipped her long blond braid over her shoulder.

"It's a free country, Klipp. Besides, don't you guys want a few minutes to digest all your food before practice?"

"She's right, guys," Chris said. "Let's order. I'm starved. But instead of my usual, I think I'll have Stretch's jumbo hot dog with the works, fries, and a Coke."

"What?" J.R. stared at Chris, his mouth wide open.

Chris winked at Stretch, and Stretch nodded back. "Yes, and I'll try J.R.'s chili with onions and cheese."

Jack chuckled. "Why not? Bring me that tuna thing, soup, and orange soda pop that Gadget always has."

"And I'll have Chris's cheeseburger, malt, and fries," Gadget added.

J.R. wasn't sure. "All right, I guess that leaves me with Jack's cheeseburger and onion rings." The gang folded their hands and placed them on the table. They turned and innocently stared up at Alex.

"In other words—the usual." Alex slipped her pencil behind her ear. "You think you can fool me. You're just going to switch the plates around after I leave them on the table."

"What makes you think that?" Chris asked, eyes wide.

"Because you guys never change." Alex shook her head and walked back to the kitchen, where she helped her dad some days after school and on weekends.

The guys laughed. "I think we had her going for a few minutes there, don't you?" Stretch said.

12

"Nah," Jack said, smiling. "But we sure gave J.R. a scare."

"You did not," J.R. fired back. "I just didn't want to get stuck ordering Gadget's tuna platter."

"We'll fool her one of these times," Chris added.

"I doubt it," Gadget said. "She's pretty smart."

"And a great pitcher," J.R. topped.

"Well, if there's nothing else," Chris continued, "all in favor of the High-Fives meeting being adjourned, say aye." He tapped his fork on the table and sat back in the booth.

Everyone except Gadget answered.

"What's the matter, Gadget?" Chris asked. "Do you have more business?"

Gadget pushed up his glasses and sighed. "No, no further business. Just once I was hoping I'd get to read the minutes of the last meeting."

He smiled and threw up his arms to surrender as the rest of the guys threw sugar packets and napkins at him.

Chapter 3

PRACTICE, PRACTICE, PRACTICE

"Hustle, hustle, hustle," Coach Ross Holton called to the outfield. "Get under those grounders. Get set and fold your mitt around the ball."

Crack. Coach Holton sent a hit into the outfield. This time the ball arced high and streaked toward Stretch. The sun was bright and blinding, but he was prepared. He figured the ball would drop short because of the stiff north wind, so he jogged forward. For a minute he couldn't find it. It must be lost in the sun, he thought. He felt his heartbeat quicken with panic. "Where'd it go?" he muttered to himself. He positioned his right arm to block the sun, and then spotted the ball already spiraling toward the ground. Quickly Stretch shifted and planted himself under the ball. He bent his knees and held both hands slightly above his shoulders. In the next

14

instant the ball smacked into the leather hollow of his glove. With a little squeeze he folded the tip of the mitt and captured the ball. "Gotcha," Stretch said with a sigh.

"Way to go, Home Run," said Chris, calling out Stretch's baseball nickname from left field.

"That's the way to do it," Coach Holton called before blowing his whistle. "Come on in."

"That was a close one," Stretch whispered to Jack as they jogged toward home base.

"I knew you'd get it, you always do," J.R. added.

"Let's just hope you always get it in the game," Jack said.

"Your faith in me is overwhelming," Stretch answered.

"Give me your attention," Coach Holton said as the team gathered and sat on the wooden bleachers at one of Conrad's municipal fields. He paced in front of his team, his medium height made taller by his long, purposeful stride. He pulled his red baseball cap down over his straight blond hair. His pale skin was already sunburned, a sign of the warm spring weather. He flipped off his sunglasses and tucked an earpiece into the neck of his blue T-shirt and let the glasses dangle. His clear blue eyes squinted against the sudden glare. "You look pretty good out there individually, but you need to start thinking and working more as a team."

"Easier said than done," Gadget muttered.

"Hey, our gang's been working as a team for over a year," J.R. said positively.

"Yeah, but there are only five High-Fives," Chris added. "There are sixteen of us on the squad."

Coach Holton flipped the first page of his roster. "Starting today we'll be having scrimmages with some of the other city league teams."

"All right," Stretch cheered. "It's like getting to play two games a week."

"Correct. Hopefully it will also give us invaluable experience and the opportunity of practicing in a game-like situation."

"And do a little spying, too, huh, Coach?" J.R. said with a twinkle.

"Precisely," Coach Holton added with a twinkle of his own. "But I prefer to call it scouting instead of spying. I want you to enjoy yourselves and have fun playing the game."

"He doesn't have much of a killer instinct," Stretch whispered to Jack.

"Maybe that's why it's still called a game," Jack answered back.

"Oh, really." Stretch kept the conversation going. "First *game* I know with multimillion-dollar contracts. Don't kid yourself, baseball's big business—"

"Not on our level," Alex interrupted. "Here it's just a game."

"Baseball takes a lot of work for a team to operate like a well-tuned machine, but that's exactly what I want us to be," Coach Holton continued. "Precise, accurate, and efficient."

16

"Maybe we should call ourselves the Robots instead of the Lions," Stretch said a little too loudly.

Coach Holton overheard the comment. "Maybe we should, but I feel the qualities of a lion fit what we should be as well. When we think of a lion, we think of a leader, aggressive, yet intelligent. The king of the jungle. I want you to think of yourselves as kings, too. Each player a king of your own territory, whether that means the king of right field, or the king of second base. Each territory is vital in order to make a strong kingdom. Defend your territory like a lion, and we'll go all the way to the city championships."

"Inspirational," Gadget said.

"Talk is cheap, we need action," Jack continued.

J.R. shrugged his shoulders. "So let's give it to 'em then."

Coach Holton blew his whistle to quiet everyone down. "Listen up. There are seven other teams and we'll need to take on each team a little differently. Today we start with a scrimmage against the Condors. Take a little time to concentrate before we start. I'll have the lineup ready when you get done warming up. Alex, lead the team in a run around the field. Not fast, just an easy rhythm to stretch out your larger muscles. After that, Jack will be in charge of the sprints between home and first. And don't forget to run through the base. Too many outs happen because a runner runs out of steam before hitting the bag. And finally, Stretch, take the bat and hit some balls. Mix it up as much as you can for fielding practice."

"No problem, Coach," Stretch answered with a smile. He loved baseball. Everything about it. The way his arms felt when the ball made contact with the bat. The smell of freshly mowed grass mixed with that of watered-down dirt on the mound and base lines. He liked being good at it, too. It had always been his sport. Instead of getting bored as he did with soccer or football, Stretch felt that each new season was exciting and made him a better player. Maybe that was why the baseball cards were so important to him, too. It was a way of keeping baseball right in his pocket, rain or shine, winter or summer. He flipped his Cubs baseball cap around backward and started to jog with the rest of the squad.

Gadget ran right behind Alex. "Condors, now that's an interesting name for a ball club."

"Can't be much stranger than Oriole or Blue Jay," Alex said over her shoulder.

"That's true," J.R. agreed. "Boy, am I glad I'm not playing for a wimpy-sounding bird team."

"Well, the condor isn't a wimpy bird," Gadget stated seriously. "It is a type of South American vulture, related to hawks and eagles."

"Now those are noble names," Stretch said, running backward a few paces. "Hawk or eagle, not vulture or condor."

"Well, the vulture is a bird of prey, aggressive and usually strong," Gadget continued his lecture.

Jack shook his head. "Yeah, but when a person is

described as a vulture, it means he's greedy or ruthless, someone who uses other people to get what he wants.''

"So, that describes a baseball team—a real group of scavengers.'' Chris chuckled.

Alex picked up the pace slightly. "Hey, don't you guys know the Condors is the team the Raiders are on?''

Stretch stopped for a minute. "Then the name really does fit.''

"Isn't Jason Fields on that team, too?" J.R. asked.

"So's Jessica White,'' Alex added.

"Man, that's tough. Two nice people on the creepiest team in the league,'' Chris said.

J.R. jogged next to Stretch. "Maybe something nice from the good guys will rub off on them.''

"Dream on,'' Jack grumbled. "If anything's going to rub off on anybody, it'll be from the Raiders. Before you know it Jason and Jessica will be knocking kids down and stealing their gear.''

"Yeah, you've heard of the Midas touch—well, they have the tin touch.'' Stretch slowed down as the group rounded the dugout.

"Speak of the devil,'' J.R. said, nodding to a group of kids moving toward them.

"Here come the Condors now,'' Alex announced. "They're early, so we can't finish our warm-ups.''

"Led by none other than Ron Porter,'' Chris added.

Jack dug the toe of his sneaker into the dirt. "Followed closely by the rest of his Raiders.''

19

"Don't you know that they're surgically connected at the hip," Gadget teased.

"Condors, Condors, help, it's the Condors." Stretch started clucking like a chicken and then cawing like a crow. Instantly Ron Porter stood taller and puffed out his chest, his freckled face tense as he glared at the High-Fives. His thick red hair bounced in the breeze, and his blue eyes were fixed on the group. On his right was Greg Forbes, a tall, skinny kid with long jet-black hair, blue eyes, and a low gravelly voice. On the other side of Ron was Randy Salazar. Everyone thought Randy was a ninth grader—he was so big and tough acting. Trailing behind those three were the two odd-balls of the group, Peter Farrell and Hank Thompson. Peter was small and scrawny with brown hair and hazel eyes. He was the smallest of the group and known as the class tattletale. And, of course, there was Hank. Stretch had always ignored Hank because he never seemed very important, not until the Mantle card showed up. Stretch would have to be careful what he did and said around him if he really wanted to do some trading. He stopped his crowing and watched as the Condors crossed the field.

"What a way to start our scrimmages," Chris said.

"Just once I wish we could do something without having those guys breathing down our backs," J.R. said with a sigh.

"And take all the fun out of competing," Jack said.

"Fun?" Alex groaned.

Ron Porter and the other Raiders had walked up to

the High-Fives now. "Gee, I'm going to love pitching a no-hitter for our first scrimmage, aren't you guys?"

"Yeah, especially to a *pussycat* team," Greg Forbes echoed.

Stretch looked to Chris. "Well, it looks like some things never change."

"Here we go again," Chris said, shaking his head. "Here we go again."

Chapter 4

BIG PLAYS

"Hey, batter, batter, swing," Condor third baseman, Greg Forbes, called. The scrimmage was in the bottom half of the sixth and the Lions were at bat. The score was seven to three, in favor of the Condors.

Jack tried to ignore Greg's banter and regripped his bat. His bat was somewhat smaller and lighter than the ones most of the guys used, but Jack hit better with it than with a bigger one.

"You call that a bat," Ron shouted from the mound. "I thought it was a pencil."

Jack glared at him and choked up on the stick. It helped him get to the ball faster. "Can it, Porter."

"Gee, if you choke up any more, Klipp, you'll have to hit the ball with your fists," Randy Salazar called from first.

Jack clenched his teeth and tried to block out the Condors' chatter. He knew if he listened much longer he'd lose it. He lost his temper easily, and they knew it. Well, this year was going to be different.

He watched the first pitch drop short, ball one. The next pitch curved away from the plate, and Jack caught a piece of it, but it spun backward and was foul, strike one.

"Stay cool, Jumpin' Jack Flash." Stretch called Jack's nickname encouragingly. "You almost had that one."

Jack shifted his weight from side to side until he felt comfortable again. He stared at the freckle-faced Porter. The next pitch was fast and the ball was released sharply, and before Jack could pull away, it smacked him in the upper arm. Jack dropped the bat and clutched his left arm. It felt as if he'd been hit with a boulder, and the rock was permanently imbedded in the bone. Jack hunched over. Coach Holton ran to home plate, followed quickly by the rest of the High-Fives.

"You okay?" Coach Holton asked.

"I could kill that guy," Jack moaned.

"He probably did it on purpose," Stretch said toward the mound.

"The guy's a maniac," Chris shouted.

"Can you move your arm?" Gadget asked.

"Yeah," Jack groaned.

"Take your base," the umpire said after blowing his whistle.

"Are you all right to play?" Coach Holton said, peering squarely into Jack's eyes.

"No problem, Coach," Jack said, changing his focus

to fix on Ron. He jogged slowly to first, shaking his stiff arm the whole way.

"Batter up," the umpire called again. "And remember, this is just a practice."

Stretch picked up his favorite bat, a Louisville Slugger he called Red Hot, for the red-hot action and success he'd had with it over the past few years. He laid it across his shoulders, draping his wrists over the ends. He twisted to the left and then whipped around to the right. His back popped once on each side. Stretch smiled. The procedure had become one of his superstitious rituals. If his back popped it usually meant a hit. Two pops meant he had a great chance of making a home run. Stretch smiled slyly at Ron as he stepped into the batter's box.

Stretch dug into his batting stance, double-checking his feet. His back foot pointed directly at the plate and his front foot aimed more toward second base in an open stance. His knees were slightly bent, and the last season he'd learned not to crouch over, so he was standing fairly straight. His shoulders and hips were level, and his weight was evenly distributed between both feet. He cocked the bat back behind his shoulder, the sweet spot about letter-high. His elbows were away from his body, and his head was still. He was ready to blast the ball out of the park. Alex was on third, so his home run would tighten the score. Then hopefully Chris could get on base, and Gadget could bring in everyone after the bases were loaded.

"Bring them home," Chris called from the dugout.

"Little hit, Evans," J.R. said. "Just get on base."

Stretch knew J.R. was right, but it didn't stop him from wanting to blast it all the way to Denver. He knew he could do it—he had the reputation of being a heavy hitter.

"Stay cool, and give it your best shot," Stretch whispered under his breath. He watched Ron like a hawk. As soon as the pitcher released the ball, Stretch automatically cocked the bat a little farther behind his shoulder, turning his hips and shoulders to give the release added power. Everything happened fast now, and Stretch hoped that his natural ability and hours of practice would pay off. His eyes were fixed on the ball as he tightened his grip. He pushed off from his back foot and stepped forward about eight inches toward Ron with the front foot. Simultaneously he whipped the stick around with a strong level swing. *Thwack*. The ball met the bat and Stretch finished with his follow-through, his right wrist coming over his left. J.R. teased him about practicing in front of the mirror in the locker room, but at least he knew he was doing things right. This year he was determined not to bail out or uppercut the ball. This was a solid hit.

"Run," J.R. shouted from the dugout.

"Go for it," Gadget added.

Stretch pushed off on the dirt and pounded toward first base. This wasn't a scrimmage for him or any of the other High-Fives. Any time they played the Raiders it was the World Series. The ball had sailed between second and third, dropping to the grass in front of Peter

Farrell at short before he had a chance to scoop it up. That gave Stretch the opportunity to beat the ball to first. Jack raced through to third, and Alex faked everyone out and was heading into home. It had been the perfect play, and the High-Fives in the Lion dugout were going wild.

"Stretch, Stretch, he's our man. He can do it, sure he can," the team chanted from the dugout.

"Way to go," Jack's voice topped the others from third.

"Nice run, Alex," Cathy Sullivan and Gadget said, high-fiving her at the dugout. The score was seven to four, and the Lions were ready to rally now. There was only one out and a runner on first and third. Chris was up to bat.

This time the outfield was quiet. J.R. patted Chris on the back. "Stay relaxed and give it to those greedy birds," he said.

"Will do," Chris said confidently. "If I don't bring them home, you guys can finish the job."

Chris grasped his favorite aluminum bat and marched up to the on-deck circle. He snapped a couple of practice swings and then jogged to the batter's box. The first ball came fast and furiously, and Chris decided it was outside. The ump saw it differently and called strike one.

Suddenly the tension of the two teams switched. The Condors heaved a sigh of relief and slowly began their banter.

"Easy out," Greg called.

26

"Don't let him shake your concentration," Gadget added quickly.

Chris stepped back to glance at the dugout and then moved back into the batter's box. The next pitch came moments later, low and inside, ball one. The following pitch was wild, and Hank Thompson, who was the Condors' catcher, dropped the ball. Stretch jumped at his chance and bolted for second base. He had a good lead-off, and good speed, but Hank had recovered the ball quickly, and it was now soaring toward second. Stretch knew he'd have to slide to be safe. A bent leg slide to beat the throw. Stretch fell to one side, extending both legs, and taking the blow on his left hip and backside, his arms still in the air. A moment later he bent his left leg, tucking it under the right. The rest of his body was straight. He felt the canvas bag hit the cleats of his shoe and the dust was thick all around him for yards. He knew he was safe. Jason, one of his friends, but also the Condors' second baseman, never had a chance to tag him. Stretch stood up and brushed the dirt from his knees.

"Nice steal," Jason said with a smile.

"Thanks. Between Porter's wild pitch and Hank's fat hands, it was pretty easy. No fault of yours," Stretch added.

Jason shrugged. "Hey, it's only practice."

Stretch smiled. Not the way I play, Stretch thought. He refocused his attention back on Chris. It was a late swing on a fast ball for strike two. "Keep your eye on it, Crackin' Chris," Stretch called, using Chris's baseball nickname.

The last pitch was almost identical to the first, and once again Porter caught Chris looking at a pitch he thought was a ball. "Strike three," the ump rang out far too clearly.

"I guess we got the out anyway," Jason said. "Rough call."

"Let's hope Gadget has better luck, I'd hate to have to steal third and push Jack home."

"Don't press your luck," Jason answered back.

The steal had shattered Ron's concentration, though. The next five pitches resulted in one strike and four balls. Gadget ran to first, thrilled to be on base so easily.

"Okay, J.R., you can win it on this one," Stretch said as he clapped his hands together.

"Grand-slam homer," Jack called from third.

Gadget was more realistic. "Little hit, big guy, just take my place."

By now both teams were calling and shouting so much that not much could be understood, but J.R. knew what he'd have to do. It was the ultimate situation. The hero or the goat. He desperately wanted to be the hero, and it was going to take all his energy to stay calm and just think about each pitch. He glanced at the fire coming out of Ron Porter's blue eyes. He wasn't thinking about Stretch's steal now. Stretch and Jack were ready to run on anything. There was only one out left, and only one inning after this to do it in if he blew it. J.R. looked at Stretch and wished he could trade places.

A hush went over the teams as the umpire blew his whistle. J.R. could feel the sweat building up on his brow and upper lip. "Please let me do this," he prayed, wiping the moisture from his hands onto his pants. It's just a practice, he tried to convince himself, but he knew better. He grasped the bat a little tighter, and looked into the outfield. He saw Stretch staring at him from second base with confidence and hope.

The first pitch was low and inside, and both teams made little reaction to the call, ball one. The second was a foul tip to right. Hank scrambled feebly to make the out but it landed with a thud in the soft dirt. One and one, the ump signaled, holding up his index fingers on both hands.

The next pitch seemed to cut the air like a glider plane through puffy clouds. There was no sound until J.R.'s bat hit the lacings. It sailed into the air slowly, traveling toward third base. It wasn't a power hit.

Greg scurried under the ball, backpedaling and calling for the catch. The left fielder moved in for backup. In the next moment Greg was under the ball, taking one more step back and catching the short pop-up with both hands. The inning was over with the bases loaded. The Condors cheered and rushed in for their last at bat.

Stretch met J.R. by the catcher's cage. "You did the best you could. It was a tough pitch."

"You would've knocked it to the next town," J.R. grumbled under his breath.

Stretch shrugged his shoulders and smiled. He picked up his outfielder's glove and jogged back to the grassy area. He wished there was something great he could've said to J.R. The High-Fives had always turned to him as their leader during baseball season, and right now he felt as if he'd been the one to strike out. He felt worse than J.R.

Chapter 5

NOMINATIONS

Chris poked his head around a row of lockers at Dugan Junior High the next day at school. "If we stay here a few more minutes we won't have to face them again."

"This is really stupid. Everybody has already gone to class," Jack grumbled.

"Do you want to see Porter and listen to more of his bragging?" Chris whispered loudly.

"No," Jack moaned. "But it still is stupid to hide out like this."

"Look, we'll get even in a real game, when it really counts. We'll slaughter them then."

"Stretch is right," Gadget added.

Stretch continued. "We just have to practice more."

Gadget glanced up at the school clock. "A lot more."

"Yeah, eight to four isn't exactly an almost win." Stretch crossed his arms over his chest.

"This is one of those days when I'm glad J.R. is still at Bressler Elementary," Gadget whispered.

"No kidding," Jack said. "The Raiders would be razzing him to death."

"Shoot, I wish I were there," Stretch said, only half-teasing.

Gadget rested his head on the redbrick wall. "Poor kid, he didn't eat a thing at Mike's afterward."

"He wasn't any better at home, either," Jack added.

"Did he talk to you about it?" Chris asked.

"Nah, are you joking. He doesn't talk to me about anything. We're not like you and your older brother Tim."

"I wish I had a brother to talk to," Stretch said with a sigh. "I'm stuck with three stupid sisters."

"Hey, who do you talk to when you get bummed, Gadget?" Jack asked. "You're an only child."

"Myself mostly," he answered.

Jack continued. "I heard J.R. calling my dad on the phone. Ever since the divorce he calls Dad when he's got anything major to talk about."

"Well, that's cool," Stretch said with a nod.

"It's hard on my mom, though," Jack added. "She thinks she's supposed to be both parents."

The bell rang, and the boys scurried to make it to their last class of the day.

"See you at practice," Gadget said as he and Jack went into the nearest classroom.

"What do you think Forbes is going to say when we

see him?'' Stretch asked Chris as he pushed open a door a little farther down the hall.

"I hope we're late enough so he won't get a chance to say anything."

"Hey, it's the Pussycats," Greg shouted from his desk in the third row.

Stretch stared at Chris before taking his seat. "Did I say he wouldn't get a chance? Fat chance was more like it."

"Late swinging at the ball, late getting to grounders, and late to class," Peter Farrell said, trying to get the boys riled up.

"Let's settle down. We have some very important business to take care of," Mrs. Sandy announced. "Today we're having nominations for school officers. As you know, every quarter each grade elects a president, vice-president, secretary, and treasurer for student council. Those elected will meet during this hour each day to conduct school business with the other grades. Each homeroom will also choose a representative, but those elections will be held after the officer elections. Since this is a high honor, and a lot of responsibility, think about your nominations carefully. The people you choose should be leaders, good listeners, and also people willing to go that extra mile to get things done."

"That's you, Stretch," Chris whispered across the aisle.

"Chris," Mrs. Sandy said. "You were vice-president first quarter, could you give us any information that might help the other students make an intelligent selection?''

Chris cleared his throat. ''Not really, except that it's fun, even though you have to work pretty hard. You get out of classes sometimes, and you get to know some of the kids in the upper grades, even though they don't talk to you that much.''

Mrs. Sandy sat at the edge of her desk. ''Thank you, Chris.''

''Just one more thing,'' Chris said, standing up again. ''I would like to nominate Stretch Evans for seventh grade president. Everybody knows him, he's not afraid of hard work, and he's funny.''

Stretch smiled broadly as the class applauded.

''All right then,'' Mrs. Sandy said, walking to the blackboard. She wrote the word *President* and Stretch's name below it. ''Anyone else?''

Greg Forbes nudged Peter Farrell, and Peter raised his hand.

''Yes, Peter,'' Mrs. Sandy said.

''I nominate Greg Forbes for president because he would be ten times better than Evans.''

Mrs. Sandy cocked her head and jotted Greg's name below Stretch's. ''Anyone else?'' She pointed to a girl sitting near the front.

''I nominate Amie Anderson,'' the girl said.

''All right, let's vote. Remember you're only voting for a nominee now, but the person we nominate from this class could be president,'' Mrs. Sandy said. ''So make your selection wisely. Close your eyes and put

34

your heads down on your desks. This is a secret ballot.''

Stretch looked over to Chris before laying his head on the desktop. "Thanks," he whispered.

"The nominations are Stretch Evans, Greg Forbes, and Amie Anderson. All in favor of Stretch raise your hand."

Stretch tried to use his hearing to detect how many votes he had. He could faintly make out the sounds of rumpling fabric and motion. He hoped the whole class was behind him. Finally he heard Mrs. Sandy write a number in chalk on the board.

"Greg Forbes," she continued. The vote didn't take as long, so Stretch thought that might be a good sign. "And now Amie Anderson." Once again Stretch tried to decipher the number of arms that shot into the air. He figured most of the girls would vote for her, she was pretty popular. "All right," Mrs. Sandy continued. Stretch could hear her wiping the board with the eraser. "You may raise your heads now."

Stretch could feel the butterflies bouncing around in his stomach. He didn't realize how much he wanted to be president until that moment. "Let it be me," he said to himself. It seemed like an eternity until Mrs. Sandy made the announcement.

"It was a very close vote, but your nominee for president will be—"

Stretch held his breath and crossed his fingers. "Please."

"Stretch Evans. His name will be added to the ten

other homeroom nominees'. Each student will receive a mimeographed list tomorrow when you get to school. You can vote for three nominees in each category. The top three will be announced in homeroom. A ten-day campaign will culminate in an election for your officers. Good luck, Stretch, I hope to see your name on the ballot after tomorrow.''

"Way to go, Evans,'' Chris cheered.

The class applauded before Mrs. Sandy continued with the rest of the nominations. Stretch could hardly concentrate on the other categories. Greg made Peter nominate him for everything but secretary. He didn't win any of them. Maybe the High-Fives weren't the only kids the Raiders picked on. It was nice to know that sometimes the bad guys didn't win. Finally the bell rang.

"Let's go tell the other guys,'' Chris said quickly, pulling on Stretch's sleeve. "They're going to want to support you in your campaign.''

"Hey, I've got to make the final cut first, you know.''

Chris laughed. "You don't have to worry about that.'' He stopped just outside the classroom door. "I can see it now,'' Chris said, waving his hand in front of himself. "Evans for President.''

"Hey,'' Stretch said, grasping Chris's other arm. "If I do make it on the ballot, will you be my campaign manager? I could sure use a man with student council experience in my corner. Besides, you're my best friend.''

"I'd be honored,'' Chris answered. "As my first unofficial act, I'll get the rest of the High-Fives to work as my assistants. We've got to get in gear.''

Stretch wanted to pinch himself he was so happy. It still shocked him to realize how much this meant to him. He'd never been interested in politics before. Usually during baseball season he couldn't think of anything but playing the game and trading cards. Now this election had given him a whole new perspective on spring training. He wanted it as much as the championship or the Mantle.

Chapter 6

THE CANDIDATES

"Jack, Gadget, over here," Chris hollered as the students flooded into the halls after school.

Gadget acknowledged Chris, and the four guys worked against the flow of the crowd to meet by the water fountain. "Before you say anything," Chris said, "just say yes."

"There's something we want to tell you, too," Gadget shouted above the crowd.

"Just say yes, first," Chris said impatiently.

Jack and Gadget turned to each other. "Okay," Jack said. "Yes."

"Gadget?" Chris said, questioning the other boy.

"I don't like to agree to something if I don't know what it is. All right, you win, but then you have to listen to me," Gadget added. "Yes. Now what did we agree to?"

Chris pushed Stretch in front of him. "You are now

looking at the next seventh grade president of Dugan Junior High.''

"Oh, dear," Gadget said with a frown.

"What do you mean, 'Oh, dear'?" Stretch asked.

Gadget was quick to answer. "Well, I think we have a problem."

Chris put his hands on his hips. "Why, what's the problem? Don't you think Stretch will make the best president?''

"Well, sure, but—" Gadget started.

"But what?" Stretch was beginning to be offended.

"I nominated, and our class voted, Jack as our nominee for president."

"Jack Klipp?" Chris said.

"What other Jack do you know?" Jack fired back.

"I didn't mean it that way. I just hadn't thought about it, I guess." Chris shrugged his shoulders.

"Well, think about it," Gadget said proudly. "Jack Klipp, seventh grade president."

"I'd like to help Jack, but I've promised Stretch I'd be his campaign manager."

"*If* I make it to the final three," Stretch added.

Chris was confident. "You'll make it. That's why I wanted you guys to say yes. You were agreeing to work on Stretch's campaign. I guess that's kind of out of the question now."

"I'll have to respectfully bow out," Gadget answered, "because I've agreed to be Jack's campaign manager when he makes the final cut."

"If," Jack said. "Stretch has a better chance of getting to the final three than I do."

"You mustn't talk like that," Gadget continued. "You mustn't even think that way. I can help you with all the experience I gained as treasurer the first quarter, but you must keep a positive attitude."

Stretch stuck his hands in his pockets. "Look, none of this is going to matter until after the final three are announced tomorrow, so why don't we drop it for now and get back to concentrating on baseball."

"Spoken like a true leader," Chris said.

"Chris," Gadget groaned.

"Sorry, I couldn't help myself," Chris apologized.

"Stretch is right," Jack said. "We can't do anything about the voting, but we can do something about hitting the ball better. Let's get out there and have a good practice."

"Words of action. He's perfect presidential material," Gadget announced, plugging his candidate.

"I thought we said—" Chris began.

"I couldn't help myself," Gadget interrupted.

"Okay, then we all agree not to talk about the campaign until after the results tomorrow. Besides, tomorrow we can vote for three people. And I, at least, know how I'm going to cast two of my votes." Stretch extended his hand and Jack smiled as he vigorously shook it.

"Spoken like a true politician," Chris mumbled.

"I've got my bike out back," Jack said, taking off

for his locker. "I'll pick up my science book and meet you guys back there."

"That's the ticket," Gadget said, patting Jack on the back. "Keep those grades up. Wait for me."

Chris glared at Gadget, then pulled Stretch toward their locker. "We'd better get our science books, too. You'll need to impress the class with your grades."

"Jack gets straight A's. I can never do that."

"He does?"

"Yeah, didn't you know?"

"Nope. It must be a well-kept secret."

"Jack wants it that way. Don't you remember how he keeps making the honor roll?"

"Jack always says its a misprint," Chris said, checking down the hall where Gadget and Jack had disappeared. "We have big laughs about it."

"Well, the joke's on you, 'cause he really is smart."

"Maybe he'll keep it secret during the campaign, too," Chris said half to himself. "We'll emphasize the all-around, honest guy angle, instead of brains."

"Are you saying I'm dumb?" Stretch asked. "Don't answer. Let's grab our bikes and get to practice."

The four boys rode over to the practice field in silence, but each one knew what the other was thinking. It could be a tough campaign if both High-Fives were on the ballot. Their mutual friends could split the ballot. Stretch secretly wished Jack were running for vice-president. It would be the perfect ticket. They'd be positive to have a landslide victory then. But that wasn't the way it was and they'd have to deal with it. All

Stretch knew was that he wanted to win bad, and he didn't want anybody standing in his way, including Jack. This was big business, just like baseball, and Stretch was in the election to win.

"Hey, Stretch," J.R. called as he pedaled across the parking lot beside the Lions' practice field. "Can I talk to you for a minute?"

Stretch snapped out of his daydream and pulled up beside a large oak tree where J.R. had stopped. "What's up?"

"I need your help."

"Sure, anything." Stretch shrugged.

"I don't want to hit a pop-up fly ball again in my life."

Stretch raised his eyes to glance over at the team gathering on the diamond. "J.R., it happens to everybody."

"Not to you. I've been thinking about it very seriously all day. I want you to coach me. Private training. I'll pay you what I can. If I run short on cash, I'll give you some of my baseball cards, I'll clean your room, work on your bike, anything. I just need some extra help."

"You don't have to pay me. I'll be glad to give you extra coaching. I can use the practice, too. But I think you should know, you *will* hit another pop-up. It happens, even to the pros. But we can meet early, stay late, or practice at my house. I've got one of those catching-batting nets in the backyard."

"Great, whatever you say. I'm willing to spend every spare hour I'm awake on this."

"Come on," Stretch said, slinging his arm around J.R.'s shoulders. "Let's go practice. Everyone's pretty much forgotten about that game."

J.R. kicked a rock across the parking lot. "I haven't and I never will."

"Well, let's go warm up." Stretch and J.R. joined the rest of the team jogging around the field. After that they did sprints and then tossed the ball around to get their arms warmed up. They stood in two lines fairly close together, facing each other. They started with easy pitches and kept moving back until the toss was about sixty feet, the distance between first and home plate, by little league standards.

Stretch felt good. His arm was beginning to get that solid accuracy he worked hard to perfect. It boosted his ego to have J.R. ask for help, too. If his name got on the ballot it would be hard finding time for everything, but somehow he'd work it out. Some things could wait if he was president of the seventh grade class. Stretch smiled; he liked the sound of that.

Prrt, prrt, prrrt. Coach Holton blasted his whistle. "Before we start on batting and fielding practice, I want to talk to you." The team gathered around. Chris sat close to Stretch.

"I've been thinking about some great ideas for the campaign," Chris whispered.

"May I have your undivided attention, please," the coach said pointedly to Chris and Stretch. "I think we learned a big lesson yesterday. The Condors are a good team and I expect them to be our toughest competition in getting to the playoffs. We'll have to play a lot better if we expect to get there. We need to work on our field play. We need to turn singles into doubles. Learn to steal a base when they least expect it. Be so sharp that each play is automatic. A little more intimidation wouldn't hurt either."

Chris leaned over and whispered to Stretch. "Listen to what he's saying, it all applies to the campaign, too."

Stretch chuckled to himself. "You mean I shouldn't steal bases."

"Very funny. I mean turning single votes into double votes, staying sharp and using some intimidation."

Coach Holton continued. "Let's mix it up a little, too. Every day that we don't have a scrimmage or a game, we're going to focus on a particular position, and drill on it. I want every one of you to be skilled in every position."

"Where have we heard that before?" J.R. said, leaning into Stretch.

Stretch remembered the year before, when Miss Hyland had coached their school team. She'd insisted on the same kind of proficiency at each position. It took a long time for Stretch to learn he couldn't just play left field, but this year it seemed natural to play all positions, and he was glad.

"Today we're going to focus on first base. Physically, Jesse is our best candidate for the position. He's tall, which makes him a good target, and left-handed, which makes the runner less likely to get in the way of the throw. But Jesse needs to work on speed and accuracy, things that Jack has. That's why they both play that position. So here's today's drill. Stretch, you'll do the batting; Cathy, take third and cover left. J.R., you're on second; Drew, take right; Tony, short; and, Michael, you'll be our runner. The rest of you take turns playing first. Line up on the foul line off first base.''

"I've always wanted to play first," Gadget said as he stood in line.

"It does keep you busy," Jack added, lining up behind Jesse.

"Yeah, action's where it's at," Chris said, tagging along. "I liked playing first last season."

"When I'm not pitching, I'd like to try it," Alex said confidently.

"The most basic drill a first baseman has is to receive throws from the other infielders to make the putout." Coach Holton stood on the pitcher's mound and gave instructions to the team. "A normal play might go like this. The first baseman sprints in front of the bag. If the throw comes directly to him he's in position to step forward with his left foot, reach as far as necessary to make the catch, and have his right toe still touching the bag. Jesse, or any other left-hander, will need to reverse the right and left feet."

"That may be hard for Jesse. I think he has two left feet," Jack whispered to Chris.

"Maybe that's why he messed up so many catches yesterday."

Coach Holton turned his attention toward Stretch. "Hit some grounders or pop flies in the infield. Michael, you run as soon as Stretch hits. Obviously the play is at first. Gadget, you're up on first."

Gadget stuck his left hand deep into the glove and smacked his right fist to groove the pocket. "Out number one coming up," he said, nodding his head.

Stretch waited for the go-ahead from Coach Holton and then tapped a hit just in front of J.R. at second base. The ball took a high bounce and Tony recovered at short. Michael, the runner, had gotten a good lead, so the play was going to be close.

"Whoa," Gadget called when he realized the ball was going to come from the right. This wasn't going to be the textbook example Coach Holton had just given. He ran in place for an instant, trying to shift his feet. He kept his left toe tucked into the corner of the canvas bag, stretching as far as he could with his right leg to reach the ball coming from Tony.

It was going to be close, and Gadget could sense Michael moving up closer on him. It was as if his breath were on the back of his neck. The ball landed in his glove, but just for insurance Gadget pulled his glove in and tapped Michael's thigh for the tag. It had been close, and not a smooth out, but Gadget had done it, and the team cheered.

Coach Holton clapped his hands. "That's what we're looking for. Michael, stay at the end of the line and, Gadget, you be the runner. Jesse, take your spot on first."

Gadget got ready to be the runner as Stretch hit a solid grounder toward Cathy at third base. "Run, Ace, run," Stretch cheered, using his friend's baseball nickname for some added incentive. Gadget dug into the dirt and powered to first while Cathy had more difficulty at third. She bobbled the ball slightly, giving Gadget the additional seconds he needed to push through the base. He was safe on first. Jesse had tried hard to get him out, but Gadget had made it in time.

"This brings us to a perfect double play situation," Coach Holton announced. "Toss me the ball, Stretch, and, Gadget, you see if you can find an opportunity to steal. In the meantime, Jesse, go home and be the runner."

Stretch stared out at the coach on the mound and waited for the pitch. He felt strange and excited at the same time. He was proud that the coach recognized him as a good hitter. He had worked hours on his batting style. It had really only been the past summer that he'd begun to direct the ball with a good percent of accuracy. A shift of the foot, a twist of the wrist, all small refinements that had made it possible for him to pick and choose where the ball would go.

"Okay, Jack, you're the first baseman. Gadget, try for the steal if you see your opportunity."

"Right, Coach," Gadget answered, excited about stealing his first base.

Jesse stepped behind Stretch to act as catcher until it was time for him to run, and Coach Holton's first pitch was inside. Stretch let it pass. Gadget took a slight leadoff, and the coach threw to Jack to bring him back to the bag.

"I'm going to get you," Jack said slyly with a smile.

"Be nice, or I won't be your campaign manager," Gadget teased back.

"A bribe?"

"This is scary," Gadget said, inching off base again, trying to steal. "I don't know how Stretch does it all the time."

Jack positioned himself on the home plate side of first base, his left foot near the foul line and his right foot just touching the corner of the base, facing Coach Holton on the mound. Practice had taught him to stay low and on the balls of his feet, his glove in front of him like a target for the pitcher. Jack glanced at Stretch and Coach Holton—he knew the ball was coming. Then all at once it happened: the ball was heading for him like a racehorse out of the gate. Gadget jumped back; Jack made the catch and lowered his glove in front of the base. He'd learned not to force the tag, since he knew he'd probably miss Gadget stabbing at him with his glove. By dropping his glove in front of the base Gadget would tag himself out as he stepped into the glove. "Yer out," Jack called.

"No way," Gadget argued. "I made it back."

"Safe," Chris said from the sidelines.

"I don't know," Alex continued. "He looked awfully close to me."

"Tie goes to the runner," Coach Holton called. "Jack, you played that perfectly. Gadget just got that extra jump back. Now you won't be afraid to take a leadoff and try stealing in a game."

"Are you kidding," Gadget gasped. "My heart's racing, my legs are shaking. I don't think I'll ever try it again." The team laughed.

The next pitch to Stretch was a little outside, right where he liked it. He wanted to smack it out of the park, but that wasn't the drill. He didn't need to prove he was a big stick to his team or himself—he'd save the grand slam for when he really needed it. For practice, he hit a hard grounder between first and second. J.R. scooped it up quickly and tagged the bag at second for the force-out, then he tossed it to his brother at first to retire Jesse as well.

"Now that's the ticket," Coach Hilton cheered.

"Whoa, that was incredible," Chris shouted.

Jack and J.R. met in between first and second and high-fived each other. "Way to play," Jack said to his brother.

"You were awesome," J.R. added, giving Jack another slap.

"Now that's the kind of double play we need in every game," Coach Holton added. "Jack, head for home, and, Chris, take your place at first base."

Stretch congratulated Jack before hitting a pop-up toward short. Tony dropped the ball in the sun, and Jack made the clear shot to first.

"Head home. You're the runner," the coach said to Chris. "Stretch, come here."

Stretch jogged out to the mound, having a pretty good

idea what the coach wanted to talk about. Stretch felt honored to be singled out. "You want me to bunt?"

Coach Hilton ruffled Stretch's short Afro cut. "You are one sharp ball player. Let's see if we can fake them out."

Stretch ran back to home, grinning from ear to ear. "Get ready to get the lead out," he whispered to Chris. "We're going for the bunt."

"Oh, man," Chris, said, sweeping his wavy blond hair under his blue baseball cap. He crouched like a sprinter getting ready for the gun.

Stretch took a deep breath, and when Coach Holton released the pitch Stretch slid his top hand up the barrel of the bat, his thumb clutching the word *red* on his "red-hot" bat. His lower hand stayed at the knob, his knuckles facing Coach Holton on the mound. Stretch tried to meet the ball and dump it between the coach and Alex on first. Chris pushed off and the chase was on.

"It's a drag bunt," Gadget called from the line.

Alex ran forward, scooping up the trickler as it rolled halfway to first. After securing it in her glove, she pivoted around and underhand tossed the ball to Coach Holton as he crossed the bag at first. Chris didn't have a chance.

Again the team went wild. It was the most exciting and tension-filled practice they'd ever had.

"Great reflexes, Alex," Coach Holton said, slightly out of breath.

"Yep," Cathy Sullivan said, running over to the

base. "She's got it all. A great pitcher, sharp at first base, and the first seventh grade female president of Dugan Junior High."

"What!" Chris said in shock.

"Alex is running for president?" Gadget said with a gasp.

Jack did a triple take. "A girl."

Stretch rubbed his forehead with his hand. "Just what I need, more competition."

Chapter 7

CUTTING A DEAL

"This is crazy," Stretch said as he picked up the list of seventh grade candidates the following morning. "Everybody who's anybody is on this list."

"It's not that bad," Chris said.

"Sure it is," Stretch continued. "The only reason you and Gadget aren't up for office is that you're not eligible. You were officers already and can't run again." He turned away. "I'll never win this election."

Gadget held up his copy of the list. "I was pretty amazed when Cathy said Alex was running."

"Who ever heard of a girl president?" Jack groaned.

Stretch leaned against his locker. "She isn't just any girl—this is Alex we're talking about."

Gadget nodded. "She'd probably do a good job."

"Whose campaign manager are you, anyway?" Jack asked.

Gadget shrugged his shoulders. "I'm just saying that

if I weren't voting for you or Stretch, I might seriously consider Alex for the job."

"Oh man," Stretch cried, shaking the list. "This is getting even worse. Did you see who's nominated from Mr. Bozeman's homeroom?"

Jack grabbed the ballot away from Stretch. "You're right, this is ridiculous. It's Ron Porter. Ron Porter is actually running for office."

"Gee, I didn't know they had a category for bully," Chris said.

"He's running for president, lame-o," Jack groaned.

"And Salazar's running for veep," Gadget said, still scrutinizing the list. "I'll bet they'll work together."

"It's too bad we couldn't have worked out something like that," Gadget said.

Chris agreed. "Yeah, Jack would have made a great vice-president."

"What do you mean Jack? I was talking about Stretch."

"You've got to be kidding," Chris fired back.

"I'm quite serious," Gadget added.

"Guys, settle down," Stretch interrupted. "We can't change it now, so we might as well face the facts and not waste our time arguing."

"Remember we're friends," Jack added.

"Jack's right. Let's just vote and not talk about it anymore. Besides, I want to talk about our card swap and Max's raffle, or maybe about our first game tomorrow."

"I guess we're a little sidetracked lately," Chris agreed.

"Okay, no more talk about the election," Gadget said.

"Until after the results last hour," Chris added. "Deal?"

"Deal," Gadget added.

Jack slammed the outside of a metal locker. "Now come on, let's go vote."

Chris held on to Stretch's arm and pulled him aside. "Wait up, I want to talk to you about something."

The others went to the cafeteria, where all the students picked up official ballots, voted, and had their names checked off the official class printout.

"Don't vote for Jack," Chris said in a whisper.

"What, are you crazy? He's one of my best friends."

"He's also some of your biggest competition. I've been looking over this list and you're right, there are some heavy hitters in this group. Porter, Alex, and Jack being the first three to come to mind. Brian Manfre and Dawn Sawada are good contenders, too. Any one of you can make it to the final three."

"Don't worry, I'm not voting for Porter," Stretch said.

Chris put his hands on his hips. "Very funny. Maybe you wouldn't vote for Ron, but he's got a lot of friends who will."

"No, he doesn't. He has a lot of enemies."

"Same difference in this game. This is politics you're in. You need all the support you can get."

"That's why I've got to vote for Jack. If for some reason I don't make it to the final three, I want to make sure Jack is on the ballot."

Chris sighed. "You don't get it. I don't mean to sound cruel, but face facts: a vote for Jack is like cancelling your own out, especially since you guys hang out together. Lots of kids will think of you guys in the same way. They'll probably only vote for one of you. You'd better make sure it's you."

"I can't do it," Stretch said. "I gotta vote for Jack."

"Okay, but don't say I didn't warn you." Chris stood in line, studying the list. "I'm voting for you, and two other people who haven't got a chance to win."

Stretch picked up his ballot and stared at the names. It was strange to see his name in print. He put a check by his name. If I don't vote for myself, it means I don't have confidence in myself—and I do, he thought. Then he paused and thought about the rest of the list. He couldn't take Chris's advice. He made his next two marks next to Jack and Alex's names. As much as he'd hate to run against them, he thought they were the best qualified for the job. Porter was another story. If he was president of the seventh grade, it would be a disaster. He shuddered. He didn't even want to think about it.

"Good luck," Miss Dixon, the librarian, said to Stretch as he handed in his ballot.

"Thanks," Stretch answered. He felt a pang of excitement as he slipped on his backpack and went outside to meet the others before the first class of the day. "Hey, J.R., aren't you going to be late for school?"

J.R. glanced at his watch. "I've got ten minutes."

"Great, how about a little baseball card trading before the bell?" Stretch asked.

"I'll listen," Chris said.

"I've still got a Fleer 1991 Ken Griffey, Jr., that's going to get interesting," Jack said.

"And I know Gadget is still interested in my Gil Hodges World Series card." Stretch fanned his stack.

Gadget rubbed his hands together. "Oh man, don't tempt me."

"Hey, here comes Thompson," Jack added. "Stretch, maybe you should try to get that Mantle again."

"Don't get him started," Chris said. "He'll be trading his twin sisters before the hour is up."

"I'd trade them now, for nothing. They're not worth the Mantle. Hey, Thompson, how about a trade?"

Hank shook his head and stood in the background.

"Too bad," Stretch said with a sigh. "You're missing the best chance you've ever had."

"I feel lucky today," Jack said. "I've got this 1990 Will Clark that's well ranked. What's anybody got that's better?"

"Is it a Topps or Upper Deck?" Stretch asked.

"Upper Deck, number five hundred fifty-six," Jack answered.

Stretch looked through the stack. "Well, my '90 Donruss Gregg Jeffries may not be better, but it's at least interesting."

"How about an even trade?" J.R. suggested, getting involved.

Jack shook his head. "Nah, I think he'll have to sweeten the pot just a little for that."

"What about your José Canseco?" Gadget suggested.

"Which one?" Stretch asked.

"The 1988 American League All-Star. Card number four hundred one."

"Hmm, maybe," Jack added. "That's the one that lists the stolen bases, right?"

"You got it," Stretch said.

Jack fingered through his pile. "Well, I've got the Rickey Henderson, Gary Pettis, and Willie Wilson in that series, and the Canseco would give me four out of the top six. Not bad."

"Sounds like a deal made in heaven to me," Chris cried.

Jack agreed. "Okay, let's trade."

"I don't believe it," Chris said with a sigh. "Somebody actually made a trade."

"I've got mine in my locker," Jack stated. "We can finalize the deal at lunch."

Stretch held his hand up. "Don't forget."

Jack smiled. "No way."

"Anybody else up for a deal?" Stretch asked, holding up his stack and looking again at Hank.

"I'll make you a deal," Ron Porter said as he and his gang walked up to the trading session. "My deal is, you give me all of your best cards and I'll give you all of my worst cards." The Raiders chuckled.

"But, Ron, all your cards *are* the worst cards," Stretch said as a quick comeback. It was the High-Fives' turn to laugh.

"Oh, really. So you're not still interested in a certain Mickey Mantle 1958?"

Stretch stood up. "That's not your card, Ron, it's Hank's."

"Maybe and maybe not."

"I thought you said you'd give me first crack at it," Stretch said to Hank, who was leaning against the brick wall.

"I've still got it," Hank mumbled.

"Yeah, but if I told you to give it to me, you would," Ron said over his shoulder to the chubby seventh grader.

Hank hung his head while Stretch crossed over to him. "You don't have to trade it to anybody," he said loud enough for everyone to hear.

"He does what I tell him to if he wants to hang out with the Raiders," Ron added.

Stretch faced Hank and extended his arm so his hand rested on the wall. "You know I want that card, but you can trade it to anybody who gives you the best deal. Keep your integrity, and don't let that creep rip you off." Stretch glanced back at Ron. "I mean it, man, don't let him run your life."

Hank raised his eyes to look at Ron quickly, but then returned them to stare at the cement walk. "Ah, he's not serious about trading today," Stretch said loud enough for everyone to hear, "but I've still got a Donruss 1987 Ryne Sandberg, card number seventy-seven. It's selling for a buck at Max's, and I'm willing to take money and or a few clever trades. I'm still looking for the 1987 Topps Don Mattingly number five hundred, or possibly a 1989 Upper Deck Mike Schmidt."

"Really?" Greg Forbes said, perking up. "You want to trade your Sandberg?"

Stretch grinned. He had the right bait. Now if he could reel in Forbes it would be the perfect way to get to Porter. "Sure, what've you got to trade for it?"

Greg flipped through his cards, frantically trying to find something that might interest Stretch. "I'm not sure I've got anything you want," Greg mumbled.

Stretch took a step closer. "Sure you do."

Greg shook back his longish black hair. "What?"

Stretch slowly smiled and looked at Ron. "Your vote."

"What?" Greg repeated.

"It's simple. I'll give you the Sandberg, and you give me your support in the campaign."

"You can't do that," Ron barked.

"That's bribery," Randy added.

"What are you doing?" J.R. asked.

"How would you know if I really voted for you?" Greg said slyly. "It's a secret ballot. No one knows how you vote."

J.R. interrupted. "Yeah, Stretch, you can't buy votes."

Stretch raised his arms. "I trust you, Greg, think about it."

"He doesn't have to think about it—it's no deal," Ron said.

"Greg can speak for himself," Stretch added. "Maybe not in front of you, but in the voting booth he's his own man. That goes for everybody. It's the way the system works."

"You're nuts, Stretch." Greg chuckled.

J.R. grasped Stretch's arm. "Can I talk to you for a minute, please?"

"Just a sec, J.R.," Stretch said, still involved in the deal. "It's up to you, Forbes. It's just like going to bat: you get a grand slam, you're happy, the coach is happy, and the team is happy. Only in our deal, you get the card, I get the vote, and the school gets the best president. See, everybody's happy."

"Do you hear what you're saying?" J.R. blurted out.

"Keep out of it, J.R.," Chris said, pulling J.R. away. "It's just politics."

"Dirty politics if you ask me," J.R. added. "This sounds like something Porter would try to pull."

Stretch walked over to J.R. and whispered, "It's a dare. A power play."

"It's not like you."

"Relax, J.R.," Stretch said, shrugging it off. "I'm just scaring Porter."

"I still don't like it."

Stretch turned his attention back to the crowd. "So what do you say?"

The groups were silent. Chris smiled slyly, waiting for the answer. Jack and Gadget huddled together in awe, but it was Ron Porter's face that was priceless. If looks could have killed, Forbes would have been a dead man. His silence meant he was actually considering the deal.

Chapter 8

AND MAY THE BEST MAN WIN

"You were awesome," Chris cheered a few minutes later after J.R. left. He and Stretch were heading to their first class. "Greg Forbes was actually considering your offer."

"I knew I wanted to win this election," Stretch said. "But I truly didn't know how much, until five minutes ago."

Chris practically danced down the hall. "You shot Porter down to size. Microscopic size."

Stretch shrugged. "Too bad Greg had already voted."

"He didn't need to admit it, though. You took a big risk. He could have really jerked your chain. What was with J.R., though? He almost blew it."

"He doesn't understand. Man, that was so exciting. For all we know, Greg did vote for me. He had three choices."

61

The boys walked to their locker and Chris opened it. "That's true, but he won't in the real election."

"I'm not going to make it till the results are read in homeroom."

Chris handed Stretch his notebook. "We'll keep your mind on other things."

"Like what?"

"The campaign."

"Isn't that a little premature?" Stretch tried not to sound too optimistic.

"Stretch, everybody I've talked to voted for you. Oh, what I wanted to tell you was that your challenge to Greg gave me the perfect theme for your campaign."

Stretch couldn't hide his excitement as he shut the locker. The boys headed for class and Stretch asked, "Really, what is it?"

"Baseball, of course. It's what everyone thinks of when they think of you. The Grand Slammer. We couldn't have a more all-American theme. We can use baseball terms in our slogans like 'Hit a home run with Stretch,' or 'It's always a hit with Stretch.' Try this one, 'Join the winning team with Stretch,' or even, oh, I like this one, 'Cast your vote for MVP, most valuable president, Stretch Evans.' "

"I like the way that sounds." Stretch stopped walking for a minute. "Hey, do you think I should use my real name for the campaign? Stuart Evans for president. It sounds more official."

Chris shook his head. "It may sound more official, but it doesn't sound like you, or our campaign."

"What do you think Jack and Gadget are going to use for their pitch?"

"I don't know, but it can't be as good as ours." The final bell rang, and Stretch and Chris slipped into their classroom.

Stretch kept losing his concentration throughout the lecture on water rights in the Midwest. He kept looking at everyone in class and wondering if they'd voted yet, and if they had, had they voted for him. Then his mind would slip into his campaign, and he visualized himself standing before the school giving his acceptance speech, thanking all the little people who had voted for him. He would also thank his opponents. It was weird to think of Jack running against him. He secretly wished Jack wouldn't make the cut. It would make it much easier to have him on his team; the High-Fives always worked together. But he knew if Jack felt a tenth of the excitement he felt, he'd want to be a winner, too. Jack was a good guy, Stretch thought. He decided he had to wish him good luck before the end of the day. Porter was a different story. If Porter made the final three, Stretch didn't even want to think about it. His stomach flip-flopped. How was he going to survive until the final class of the day?

The hours before lunch moved at a snail's pace and Stretch tried several times to talk with Jack alone, but somehow they were always interrupted. Now it was the last class of the day and the final results were minutes away. Stretch sat at his desk, his fingers gripping the top where the wooden edge met the green metal frame. Every eye was on him, or at least he felt that way.

Mrs. Sandy turned the room intercom on to listen to the results. "I'd like to wish all of our nominees good luck," she said.

Chris leaned across the aisle and gave Stretch's arm a punch. "Here goes, big guy."

"Thanks," Stretch said, forcing a smile. He couldn't believe how nervous he was. He remembered Gadget saying how nervous he felt before each game. Stretch gulped down the lump in his throat. He'd never survive one season. He'd have to remember to be more sympathetic to Gadget in the future.

"May I have your attention, please," the voice said over the small box tucked into the upper right-hand corner of the room. It was the vice-principal. "We have the results of the class election primaries. I'll begin with the seventh grade secretary finals."

Stretch didn't hear a word, except Kaitlyn, the girl representing his class, was one of the final three, and Stretch jumped when the class, cheered as her name was called. No one they knew well made it for treasurer, but Randy Salazar had made the cut for vice-president. Chris and Stretch exchanged glances as Greg and Peter shouted hooray from their desks.

"Too bad," Stretch said to Scott, the boy who was the veep candidate from their class. "I voted for you."

"Thanks, maybe next time," Scott answered.

Stretch could read Scott's emotions like a book. The disappointment was all over his face. This was awful, he thought. Why did there have to be losers? He'd never been so sensitive about competition before, but somehow this was different. Losing a game was always a bummer, but you got the chance to redeem yourself the next week. There really wasn't a second chance in this game. You'd be tagged a loser.

"And finally, the candidates for president of the seventh grade class," the vice-principal called. "Jack Klipp."

Chris and Stretch automatically looked at each other. They were happy but a little surprised. Jack was a good friend, but until he'd been with the High-Fives, he'd always been considered kind of a tough guy loner.

The vice-principal continued. "Ron Porter."

"Drat," Chris said, making a fist and lightly pounding it on the desktop.

Simultaneously Greg and Peter cheered.

There was a slight pause in the announcement. Stretch clutched his fists so tightly he could feel his fingernails dig into the fleshy part of his palms. "The third candidate is Alex Tye."

Stretch bit his lower lip and tried to control the adrenaline that was searing through his veins. He felt embarrassed and ashamed at the same time. He stared blankly at the desktop. Ten seconds had gone by, but it felt like an eternity.

"We have a unique situation here," the vice-principal continued. "Two of the nominees had the exact same number of votes, so we have four presidential candidates. The fourth candidate is Stretch Evans."

Stretch bolted to his feet, shooting his right arm into the air. "Yes," he shouted. "Yes, yes, yes."

Chris met him in the aisle and high-fived his candidate. "We did it. I knew you'd make it."

"I can't believe it, I thought I was a goner."

Mrs. Sandy stepped in front of her desk. "Congratulations, Stretch and Kaitlyn, I hope you have successful campaigns."

Stretch's grin covered his face. He'd done it. The campaign was just beginning, and already he felt victorious.

"We should have a rally after school today," Chris said as he sat down.

"We have practice for the game," Stretch said back.

"I've been asked to read this announcement to all the candidates," Mrs. Sandy said. "There will be a brief meeting immediately after school today in the auditorium. Campaign rules, budgets, and dates will be explained."

For the rest of the class, Stretch didn't hear a word. All he could remember was his name being called as the fourth presidential candidate. Finally the bell rang and the class poured into the hall. Stretch looked over the heads of most of the students. He was looking for Jack.

"Hey, Klipp," Stretch called over the noise.

Jack waved his arm back. "Pretty amazing."

Stretch pushed ahead of Chris and tugged Jack into an empty classroom. "I need to talk to you a minute."

"Sure, what's up? I'm not voting for you no matter how many baseball cards you give me," Jack cried.

"No, it's nothing like that. Look, I want you to know that I think it's great you're running. It's going to be hard competing against you. Since we probably won't be having this chance again, I wanted to wish you good luck. I think you'd make a great president, so let's not let this campaign hurt the High-Fives. Deal?"

Jack stood quietly and smiled at Stretch. "Deal."

"And may the best man win." Stretch added.

Chapter 9

THE COST OF WINNING

"Sorry I'm late," Stretch said as he ran into the back-yard of the Evanses' brick colonial-style home. "I had to stay for another election meeting after school."

J.R. set his bat down. "That's okay. Your mom gave me some cookies, and I've been swinging the bat. I'm really excited about our first game tonight. So, do you like running for president? Is it weird competing against Jack?"

"Well, I wish it were different, but it's not," Stretch added as he slipped on his glove. "It's nothing personal. Does Jack have a great campaign strategy ready to go?"

"I don't think so. He and Gadget were up pretty late last night working on something, though."

"I see." Stretch tried to hide his growing curiosity. "I'm using baseball as my theme. You know, posters, cards, slogans." He pretended to be an umpire. "Things like, 'Play it safe and vote for Stretch for president,' stuff like that."

"Cool," J.R. added.

"I'm having a campaign party at ten tomorrow morning. It should last a couple of hours. Why don't you come over, then we could go over to Max's for the raffle after that."

"I—I don't know," J.R. stammered. "About the campaign party, that is."

"Oh, you mean because you don't go to Dugan?"

"Well, that, but mostly because of Jack. Besides, I can't vote, you know, so I thought I'd try to stay out of it."

Stretch ruffled J.R.'s hair. "It doesn't matter if you can't vote. You can come over to hang out if you want. I thought you might be interested."

J.R. smiled. He was glad Stretch was still including him in things. "I'll think about it, but to be honest, right now I'm more interested in tonight's game. After that scrimmage with the Raiders, I've been feeling shaky."

"No sweat," Stretch said, moving his four-foot-by-five-foot practice net into place. "We'll try a couple of things and you'll be feeling better in no time."

"Just as long as it's in time for this game."

Stretch shimmied the net into its final position about ten feet from the tall wooden fence that enclosed the Evanses' backyard. "Let's practice a couple of catches first. I want to watch your technique. Stand about twenty feet back. Toss a few into the net and then go for them.''

"Okay," J.R. said. He threw the first ball at the top of the net and it sprang back like a grounder. J.R. centered himself and scooped it into his glove.

"Don't wait for it," Stretch instructed. "Charge the ball. If it's anything but a pop-up, be aggressive and run up to it. Get down low and let the ball slide into your glove. If nothing else you'll intimidate the runner.''

J.R. threw the ball into the net again. This time when the grounder came back to him he was on top of it. "Much better. Now you're living up to your nickname, Dogcatcher," Stretch called. "Now try a series of fast plays. When the ball hits your glove, take it out and fire it at the net again. Let's get that blood flowing."

The first two came back low, but the third one that J.R. had pitched into the center of the net came back high and spinning. "Run back and get under it," Stretch instructed. "Don't underestimate a hit."

J.R. ran back, keeping his eye on the ball. It lost some of its power and dropped lightly into J.R.'s glove. "Got it."

"Pretend you have to get it to second base. Use a snap throw, you know, quick with the wrist."

J.R. set it soaring with a lot of force, but his accuracy was way off, and the ball smacked against the wooden fence instead of the net. "Sorry."

Stretch ran after the ball. "That's why I set the net up this way instead of facing the house, no windows."

"Thanks, I appreciate it, and I'm sure your mom does, too."

"So maybe we need to work on your accuracy for a while. You need to relax. It's a long way from center field to the pitcher."

"But I'm usually catcher."

"True, but you never know when you might be forced to play the outfield. Besides, the same rules apply. Remember the passed ball in the game against the Raiders?"

"It was a wild pitch," J.R. said, defending himself.

"Come on now, J.R., think about it. The official scorer would have charged you with the passed ball, not Alex with the wild pitch. That doesn't mean that sometimes it might not be her fault, but either way you need to be able to recover and recover fast."

"You're right," J.R. answered, lowering his head.

"Look, you've got a lot of pressure playing catcher. You're in on each play. Hey, when I'm in the left field, I can go a whole inning without touching the ball." Stretch tossed him the ball. "You can use that to your advantage. Your eyes should be so used to judging pitches that your batting average could be one of the best in the league."

"Well, it's not."

"Then let's change it. When Alex pitches today concentrate on what the pitch is doing. Is it a fastball that rises or is it a change-up? Maybe it's a breaking pitch curve ball or a slider. I'll bet you can even tell if a guy is going to strike out."

"I should be able to," J.R. said as he switched the ball from hand to hand. "But I can't."

"Now don't get bummed. Let's talk about playing catcher for a minute. What do you see your job as?"

J.R. scratched his head. "Well, it's tough. It's not easy squatting for a long time. Sometimes my legs and especially my knees get tired, not to mention having to wear all that equipment on a hot day."

"I hear ya."

"Sometimes it's really frustrating because I can see lots of things happening at one time."

"That's because you're the only player who's facing that direction."

J.R. was on a roll now. "And I have to deal with the coach and the pitcher. Now, Alex is great, but when Jack's pitching he never wants to do what I tell him. Giving signs is hard, too. I've got to block them from the first base coach with my knee and glove, not to mention trying to catch every ball so it looks like a strike."

"Take it easy, take it easy, I believe you. I'd be a lousy catcher; that's why the coach never asks me to play there. But you're good at it, and I'm here to help you get even better and match your potential."

"Sorry," J.R. said, settling down. "If I were a seventh grader, it'd be different. It's just that sometimes I get so frustrated trying to keep up with you guys."

"Then quit trying. Besides, when we're over the hill, you'll have at least one good year left." The boys laughed, and Stretch put his arm around J.R.'s shoulder. "Look, it's like what we tried to tell Gadget during football season. You don't have to be a pro, you just have to do your best. No one expects you to hit a grand slam every time you go to bat. It may sound corny, but that's all that anybody can ask of you. It's when you stop trying that people jump all over ya."

"Okay, I'll chill out for a while." J.R. picked up a bat. "When I start hitting better, I'd like to try batting left-handed, too. It should make me more valuable."

"Sounds good. I'm going to throw you some so you can practice hitting, and then we'd better get to the game."

By the time Stretch and J.R. made it to the field, the rest of the team was already playing pepper, tossing the ball around.

Chris ran up to the pair. "Where have you guys been? It's not a good idea to be late when you're running for public office." Chris pulled Stretch aside and let J.R. continue to the dugout. "I fixed it so there would be a lot of kids here for you to impress today. The school photographer may even show up, so next time you're going to be late, let me know."

"You sound like my mother. We were practicing at my house," Stretch said.

"Well, I don't mean to sound cold, but you can't afford to spend too much time with a nonvoting individual."

"This is J.R. we're talking about."

"It's only for ten days. You want to win, don't you?"

"Yeah, b-but—" Stretch stammered.

"Just do it. Oh, and I thought you might sign autographs after the game. Maybe you can make a speech, nothing fancy, just casual and cool."

"You want me to make all the outs, too, I suppose."

"Well, it wouldn't hurt, especially since I told them you'd make a home run, preferably a grand slam."

Stretch's mouth dropped open. "What? I can't guarantee that."

"Ah, it's no sweat for you."

Stretch grabbed Chris's arm. "Stop making promises that I can't keep."

Meanwhile, back in the dugout, Jack and Gadget were grilling J.R. for answers.

"So what did he tell you?" Gadget wanted to know.

Jack put his face right next to J.R.'s. "Did he make any slipups on his campaign strategy?"

"No, we didn't talk about the election. We talked about baseball," J.R. said.

"He's sneakier than we thought," Jack continued. "Now think back, are you sure you didn't tell him anything?"

"I didn't know anything to tell. He just asked me if I wanted to come to his poster party tomorrow."

"What a sneak," Jack added, focusing on Stretch warming up across the field.

"He's trying to get you to work against your own brother."

"It wasn't like that at all. He asked as a friend."

"Right."

"Well, he's not going to make a fool out of me,"

Jack said, glaring again. "You're not going near his house again."

"You can't tell me what to do."

"I always have before," Jack stated.

"It's for political purposes only," Gadget tried to explain. "It's not a good policy for you to be seen with one of Jack's opponents. The voters might get the wrong idea."

"The wrong idea about what? That Stretch and I are good friends. That he's willing to take some extra time to help me improve my ball game. Guys, I can't vote, but even if I could, you have no right to tell me who I can or can't hang out with."

"We're not trying to do that," Gadget said.

"It sure sounds that way to me."

"Look, this is politics. If I can't outdo him, he'll outdo me. Stretch isn't as honest as he seems. Didn't you learn anything from that card deal he tried to pull on Greg? The only thing he cares about for the next ten days is votes."

J.R. shrugged. "No way. The thing with Forbes was a dare."

"Wait and see," Jack said with a smirk. "He's just going to use you to make me look bad."

"I don't believe you," J.R. said. "In fact I'm going over to him right now, and I bet he gives me all the attention I need." J.R. walked across the field where Stretch had stopped batting practice to talk to some kids. "Hey, Stretch," J.R. called. "How about a little catch?"

Chris intervened. "He's kind of busy right now, J.R. Why don't you try later."

Stretch glanced at Chris then back at J.R. and shrugged. "Sorry."

J.R. turned around and looked at his brother and Gadget. They'd seen the whole thing. He dug his toe into the dirt. Maybe they were right.

Chapter 10

GAME STRATEGY

Stretch held the bat firmly, his right hand above the left, his grip lower than usual. His head and body were very still and straight. It was the fifth inning of the Lions' first baseball game, and the team couldn't have asked for more. The score was Lions eight, Comets two, and Stretch was thrilled with the great opener they were having. It was a big difference from their scrimmage with the Condors. Today Stretch had hit a homer, two singles, and a triple, and now he was up to bat again. It was hard not to become overconfident. Stretch had to remind himself that each time at bat was different and that this time he could strike out as easily as he could hit a home run.

"Come on, give me my pitch," Stretch muttered to himself. The pitcher seemed to be shifting his weight a lot, so Stretch concentrated even harder on the ball. The ball released and the pitch was low and inside.

"Ball one," the umpire called.

"You're not going to walk me," Stretch said loud enough for the catcher to hear.

"We should," the catcher answered.

The next pitch was a fastball, but Stretch's timing was sharp and he went for it. In one fluid motion his body moved into the ball, which was high and outside. His top wrist rolled over his bottom one, and he met the ball slightly in front of the plate. His legs were still planted firmly in the back of the batter's box, and he swung as hard and level as he could. His follow-through brought his body to a complete turn, and he powered the ball toward first.

"Go, Stretch, go," the Lions' bench cheered.

It was a fast start, his eyes focused on the canvas first base bag. The ball bounced by the first base foul line, but Stretch had already touched the inside of the bag, rounding first and aiming for second. He had a stand-up double, and felt great.

The fans in the stands waved their posters and banners that had various slogans cheering Stretch for president. Stretch smiled and returned their calls with a "woo, woo" and a circle arm swing. He loved this game.

"Way to go, Pres," a group of seventh graders said from the stands.

Stretch liked the way that sounded and gave the group the thumbs-up sign. He glanced at Jack and Gadget in the dugout. They looked unimpressed, but Chris smiled, knowing their strategy was working.

"Come on, J.R.," Stretch called as the younger Klipp brother did a few practice swings in the air. Stretch hoped that their practice session would help. He felt bad about not talking to him right before the game, but now that he was running for president, he had to spread himself out a bit.

J.R. didn't acknowledge Stretch, but pulled the front of his cap down and choked up on the bat. "You're not the only hotshot, Evans," J.R. muttered to himself.

"Make it an even ten," Chris shouted.

"Just get on base," Gadget instructed.

"Strike one," the umpire called as the first pitch caught J.R. unprepared.

"Shake it off, Dogcatcher," Jack called to his brother.

J.R. nodded and waited for the next pitch. The pitcher released the ball. And when J.R. saw it coming too close to the inside, he bailed out and fell back into the dirt.

"Hey, take it easy," Jack called again.

"Watch what you're doing," Alex shouted.

Gadget squinted into the sun. "Are you all right?"

J.R. stood up, slowly brushing dust from his jeans. He tucked in the new orange and blue T-shirt that the team had just gotten. He nodded to the umpire and stepped back to shake out his shoulders. He needed to relax. The count was only one and one; he could afford to take his time.

"Get back in there," Jack said firmly.

"Remember practice," Stretch added.

Stretch could tell the Comets' pitcher was just as shaken by the jam pitch as J.R. was. Now was the perfect time to steal third. It would be impressive, he thought, and I doubt if I'd get caught, but on the other hand they did have rather a commanding lead and he didn't want to get the label of being a bush player. Confidence was one thing, bragging was another. He could impress the voters, but he hated grandstanding. He settled back and decided to watch J.R. and evaluate the next pitch.

The pitcher had a smooth release and a second strike was called. "Drat," J.R. said, stepping out of the batter's box again.

"No problem," Stretch shouted. He knew J.R. would be getting nervous.

"Hang in there," Jack topped.

J.R. stepped back in, and this time he looked serious. His eyes were fixed on the ball in the pitcher's hand. He double-checked each muscle and dug in. "I'm ready for you this time," he said.

The catcher sent a signal, and moments later the ball whizzed within view. J.R. stepped forward and put his weight into the fastball. The end of the bat connected with the leather surface and J.R. sent it into the pocket between short and center. Stretch had gotten a great jump on the pitch and was rounding third and concentrating on home plate. Meanwhile, J.R. ran through first base, easily beating the throw.

"Yeah," J.R. cheered.

"I knew you could do it," Stretch called from home.

The fans went wild and Stretch tipped his hat to the crowd. They began chanting "Stretch for president," and Stretch took a bow.

Jack ignored the attention and brushed by Stretch as he stepped up to bat. Get ready to run, he seemed to signal to J.R. He didn't hesitate or blink, but swung and connected on the very first pitch. Unfortunately it was a pop-up, and Jack was out before Alex had even stepped into the on-deck circle.

The Comets were inspired for a big rally and Jack's quick out seemed to be the first incentive they'd felt all game. The third baseman began the around-the-horn, the ball going from third to second to first and then back to the pitcher.

"That's okay," J.R. tried to reassure his brother. "You'll get them next time."

Jack shoved his bat back into the barrel outside the dugout. He wanted to kick the fence, scream at the pitcher, or maybe walk away. Instead he sat at the end of the bench and hid his head in his hands.

"It was a freak accident," Stretch said as he sat next to him on the bench. "That was the first good pitch that guy's had all day."

"Don't bother sweet-talking me." Jack couldn't hide his sarcasm. "I suppose you would have turned it into a home run. Or maybe your campaign manager paid off the pitcher to make me look bad."

"What?" Stretch stood up and stepped back. "Come on, Jack, you don't mean that."

"I wouldn't put it past you guys. First you try to turn

my brother against me, and then I have this incredibly bad day on the field against a team that's going to end up in last place."

"Take it easy, Jack," Stretch whispered.

"Don't tell me to take it easy." Jack pushed Stretch's shoulder.

"Hey, it was only an out, not the end of the world," Chris added, stepping between the two.

"Yeah, but with all those kids out in the park, it could be the end of my campaign. Who's going to vote for me now?"

Gadget tried to calm Jack. "They're not voting for a baseball player, they're voting for a president. We'll make sure they know the difference."

Thwack. Alex had connected on a full count and the ball was sailing over the fence.

"It's gone, bye-bye," Cathy cheered.

The High-Fives quit arguing long enough to watch Alex run out the bases. J.R. stepped into the dugout after stepping on home plate, and dished out a series of high-fives to Alex and Cathy. "What is going on in here?" he asked.

"Nothing," Jack said, returning to his spot on the bench.

"Nothing? I could hear you guys arguing on first base."

"It's over now, forget it," Stretch said back.

"Look, if this is about the election, you guys better wise up, 'cause from an outsider's viewpoint the only one who doesn't look like a jerk right now is Alex, and if I could vote today, that's who I'd be voting for.

Stretch shook his head. "What'd I do?"

Jack groaned.

"If you don't know," J.R. said quietly, "I'm not going to tell you."

Chapter 11

TRADING FRIENDS

"You were great, Stretch," Lisa, a girl from Stretch's class, said after the game. "May I have your autograph?"

"Only if you promise to give him your vote," Chris answered.

"No problem there," Lisa said, searching for something Stretch could sign. "Ah, gee, I don't have anything for you to write on."

"Here, use this." Chris grabbed Stretch's backpack and pulled out one of Stretch's baseball cards and shoved it into his hands. "Sign this."

Stretch turned the card over in his hands nervously. "Pretty good card, Kevin Maas. It's not worth a lot, but the guy's decent. I hear his brother is, too."

"Just like our candidate," Chris said, patting Stretch's shoulders.

The girl left and three other kids came up to Stretch wanting to congratulate him on the Lions' first win.

Chris jumped into action and started handing baseball cards to all the fans. Stretch signed them, and Chris encouraged them to stick safety pins in them and wear them throughout the campaign.

"And don't forget to come to my house tomorrow morning at ten," Stretch cried.

"Yeah, we're making posters," Chris hollered after them. "This is a great idea," Chris continued. "Do you have any more spare baseball cards at home?"

"Stacks of them," Stretch said. "But before you start giving them away, let me go through them and keep my favorites. I was kind of sorry to see the Maas go. Let me use my duplicates, I can fill a room with those."

"How about filling a school, or rather a class of seventh grade voters. If we could get all the seventh graders to wear an autographed Stretch Evans baseball card, everyone would know you're the best candidate for president."

"Well, I've got a ton of them, except I was going to take them to trade at Mike's and then at Max's. Which reminds me, shouldn't we get going—we told Gadget we'd be right over at Mike's."

Chris grabbed Stretch's arm. "You can't trade any cards, we need them for the election."

"I have to trade," Stretch said.

"Okay, you're right. If you're put into a position to trade, do it. Even if it's a bad trade, go along with it. We can't handle any bad publicity."

"It was my idea to have the trade at Mike's in the

85

first place, and I'm not going to give away my best cards 'cause it might look bad for me as a candidate.''

"Well, then, tell them you've changed your mind. Pretend you're not interested in trading. You can bluff them."

"Jack and Gadget are going to be hard to bluff. They'll know something's up if I'm not out there swapping. If you hadn't noticed, they don't trust us much these days." Stretch put his cards back in his pack. "Yeah, I thought Jack was going to lose it during the game."

"He wasn't much better after the game," Chris added. "He's just jealous because our campaign is going better than his."

"Well, I don't know about that."

"The facts talk. You had twice as many followers at the game today than he did. More banners, everything. I think it really bugged him."

"It didn't seem to bother Alex. She was hot on the mound and with a bat."

"Alex isn't our competition—Jack is," Chris said, leading Stretch off the field. "And I suppose Porter, but I think we should focus on Jack."

Stretch smiled. "Well, you're the boss. I don't like ignoring J.R., though. I need to talk to him."

"Sure, but make it quick, you've got to socialize."

A few minutes later Stretch and Chris were mingling with the other traders at Mike's.

"Nice of you guys to show up," J.R. said over the crowd. "What kept you?"

"Oh, just some personal election business," Chris said.

"I'll be glad when this thing's over," J.R. said. "Gadget and Jack stormed out of here a few minutes ago."

"You're kidding. Why?" Stretch asked.

"They said something about this whole thing being an election party for you."

Stretch stood stunned. "What?"

"It's not, is it?" J.R. asked. "Just because you're using baseball as your theme doesn't mean everything with baseball was planned by your campaign manager."

"Exactly," Chris said as he slapped his hands on his thighs.

"Would you sign my baseball card?" a girl from Stretch's English class asked.

"Sure," Stretch said, reaching into his backpack for a pen.

"Or maybe Jack wasn't so far off," J.R. said, pulling on the brim of his cap.

"What am I supposed to say?" Stretch asked.

J.R. couldn't hide his disappointment. "How about, 'I'll trade you a McGee for a Clemente.' "

"Look, J.R.—" Chris started.

"No, you look," J.R. continued. "Gadget and Jack said you were out only to win, and I didn't believe them. I thought this trade was supposed to be for fun, not politics."

"It is," Stretch said. "If you'll remember, we set up this trade before I was even nominated."

"Somehow, it's gotten all turned around," J.R. mumbled.

Stretch sighed. "Well, don't blame me."

"I'm not really. It's just that this election is getting in the way of the High-Fives." J.R. shrugged his shoulders.

"Come on, Stretch, there are some potential votes over here," Chris said.

"I got to go," Stretch said reluctantly. "I'll talk to you in a little bit."

"I think I'll leave. I'll see you tomorrow."

"At my house?" Stretch asked eagerly.

"Nah, I don't think so," J.R. said, not meeting Stretch's eyes. "I'll see you at Max's."

"Come on, J.R., stay," Chris said, following him. "We've been looking forward to this for a long time."

"Hey, Stretch, how's it going?" Jason from the Condors asked. "I hear you're up for some hot trading. I've got a Fleer 1989 Wade Boggs I'll trade for an '89 Donruss Gregg Jefferies."

"W-well," Stretch stammered. He wanted to convince J.R. to stay, but he didn't want to ignore Jason either. "Let me look it up in the Beckett. You want to help?" he asked J.R.

"Not today," J.R. answered. "See you around."

Stretch lowered his head. "See you."

"So what was the trade you wanted?" Chris said, refocusing his attention on Jason. He pulled out Stretch's Beckett card catalog and handed it to Stretch.

Stretch flipped to the page. The Jefferies was a much

more valuable card. "I don't know, Jason. It's not exactly a fair trade."

Chris pulled Stretch away. "Do it. Remember Jason plays on Porter's team, and we could use him in our corner."

Stretch groaned. "Okay, Jason, it's a deal." He reluctantly handed Jason the card as he peered out a window to watch J.R. walk away.

Chapter 12

HOT TRADING

"Ta-da," Chris said, holding up a campaign poster. "What do you think?"

"It looks great," Stretch answered.

"How's that twenty-foot banner coming along?" Chris asked a group working in the corner of the Evanses' recreation room.

"Fine, we just hope we don't run out of blue paint before it's done," one of the supporters replied.

"Don't worry about it. You'll be able to read it no matter what color it is," Chris said. He walked over to the long strip of butcher paper that several kids were working on. " 'We're voting for Stretch Evans for seventh grade president,' " he read from the banner. "All the kids are going to sign it, and other kids can sign it during the campaign. Pretty clever, huh?"

"Perfect," Stretch agreed.

Eric, one of the workers, stood next to Stretch.

"It'll have three hundred names on it before election day."

"That should just about do it," Chris said proudly.

"Yeah, it'll be the in thing to do," another boy added.

"Jack and I are going to hang it up first thing Monday morning."

"A couple of the guys have volunteered to hang the baseball posters, too," Eric said.

"The one with Stretch's face superimposed on all the baseball cards is going up on the gym door. It's the best."

"The Cal Ripken one is hysterical."

"Not as funny as the Nolan Ryan."

"Yeah, using the Polaroid was a stroke of genius," Chris said.

"Do you think we're sending the wrong message by changing the faces?" Jack asked.

Chris shook his head. "Nah, it emphasizes Stretch's sense of humor."

"Plus, it gets his face all over the school," Eric added.

"Hey, was that the front doorbell again?" Stretch asked. He bounded up the stairs from the recreation room to the front door. "Maybe it's J.R.," he called back to Chris.

"Don't count on it," Chris mumbled.

Stretch opened the door, but no one was around. He craned his neck to look in all directions.

"What are you doing?" Jasmine Evans, Stretch's younger sister, asked.

"I thought I heard the doorbell," Stretch replied.

"Oh, it was probably just one of the twins. When are all your goofy friends leaving?"

Stretch leaned up against the doorjamb. "They're not goofy. But if you really have to know, they're leaving at one."

"Won't be soon enough for me."

"I've got to get over to the raffle at Max's."

"Oh, great, just what we need, more baseball junk."

"It's not junk. Some of these cards are worth a lot of money. If I win the raffle, I could own a Brooks Robinson '65, or a '64 Hank Aaron; he's even got a '62 Willie Mays."

"I'd rather have a new outfit," Jasmine said, walking into the kitchen and opening the refrigerator door.

"You're just jealous."

Jasmine poured a class of juice and started out of the room. "Of you? Of baseball cards? Get real."

"I might even make the trade of my life," Stretch called after her. "One of the guys said he might trade his Mickey Mantle." He followed her out into the hall.

"Hey, Stretch, who was at the door?" Chris yelled up to him.

"Nobody," Stretch answered. "It was just Jazzy making a lot of noise." He went back down the stairs. "I was kind of hoping it would be J.R. I feel bad about yesterday."

"Look, he'll forget all about it after the election. Jack will get used to you winning, and J.R. will forget about the stuff they said."

"I guess so," Stretch said with a sigh.

"Hey, look, it's getting late, Let's wrap this up and get over to Max's," Chris said, checking his watch. "I've got to buy something so I have a chance to win. Plus, we have to be present to win, you know."

"I know. That's why I bought all that stuff yesterday. I have twelve chances of winning today. Thompson said if he didn't win the Hank Aaron and I did, he'd consider an even trade for the Mantle. I feel lucky."

"Well, don't count on Hank's following through. Porter's got him on a short leash, and he's probably got something up his sleeve."

Stretch said goodbye to all the volunteers and began to put the paint supplies in a big box in the corner. "Why would he do that?"

"Why does Porter do anything?"

Stretch grabbed his baseball cap. "Well, I'm not going to worry about it until it happens. Let's just get over there."

"Okay, okay, we're all finished here for today," Chris said to the last few stragglers who'd helped clean up. "Thanks a lot for your help. Just keep it up all week and don't forget to vote."

"We're heading over to Max's Swap Shop if anyone's interested in doing a little trading," Stretch added.

"Look at all these people," Stretch said as he and Chris parked their bikes outside Max's Swap Shop. "Do you think all these people are here for the raffle?"

"What did you expect? You're not the only trader in town, you know. Besides, Max's is *the* trading place."

"I know, but I didn't think there'd be this many. Have you seen any of the High-Fives?"

"Nah, but I think I recognized Gadget's ten-speed on the other side of the bike rack. Let's see if we can push through the crowd and get inside."

The boys elbowed their way around a couple dozen customers jamming the aisles of Max's small, cluttered memorabilia shop. Stretch couldn't believe there was such a following for baseball cards. There were old people, businessmen, and kids from Dugan and other schools.

"Hey, there's Hank Thompson," Stretch said, making his way toward the chubby boy. "We still on for a trade if I win the Hank Aaron?"

"You got it," Hank answered, checking over his shoulder. Stretch guessed it was for Ron. "My dad said he named me after Hank Aaron, so I think I'd better get it."

"Well, I'll be happy to accommodate you." Stretch patted Hank's shoulder. "See you later."

The boys walked around until they saw the back of Gadget's sandy hair.

"Hey, what's happening?" Stretch asked as soon as he reached him.

"Not much. Max announced the raffle would be in about ten minutes. I think he's milking this for all it's worth."

"How do you mean?" Stretch asked innocently.

Jack interrupted. "He said he'd have the raffle at one and it's one-fifteen now. I think he just wants to get a couple more sales in."

"Well, hey, it's business. Why else would he give away some of his best cards?" Chris said matter-of-factly. "I'd better go get that Topps All-Star group I've been looking at."

"From the looks of things," Stretch said, gesturing to the crowd, "he's made a bundle today. Let alone the past week."

"Well, I'll never win," J.R. said, pushing up to them. "I had no idea baseball cards were such big business."

"It's a multimillion-dollar operation," Stretch said. "And after today, when I win the Mays, Aaron, and Robinson, I'll be a millionaire, too."

"What a dreamer," Jack said and chuckled.

"I'd like to think of it as confidence," Stretch added quickly.

"Just like winning the election," Chris added.

"Now that's a dream. Weren't you on your way to buy something, Chris?" Gadget asked.

"It can wait. Stretch isn't a dreamer. He's realistic."

"Then I think you should think realistically," Gadget said with a shrug.

"I am." Chris defended his stand.

"Look, guys"—J.R. tried to intervene—"you're not going to solve this here. It's all going to depend on the election Friday. Your seventh grade class will decide."

Gadget pushed up his glasses. "I just don't like the way you make it sound all the time."

"Make what sound?" Chris quizzed.

"Like Stretch is the *only* candidate for president."

"In my mind he is."

Gadget crossed his arms over his chest. "Well, in my mind, Jack is better suited for the job."

"You can't mean that," Chris stated.

"I do," Gadget said. "Everyone underestimates Jack's abilities. He's smart, and tough, which is also a good quality. He's also very realistic. He'll look at and work on the hard problems that seventh graders face. And he won't think of winning as another trophy to display with a bunch of stupid baseball awards."

"Are you saying that Stretch only wants to be president to be more popular or to get an award?" Chris asked.

"Well, you have to admit that Stretch likes being the center of attention, and being seventh grade president would certainly accomplish that," Jack added.

"All right. That's enough," J.R. cried. "You'd better stop before someone says something he can't take back."

"I'm not saying anything that everybody doesn't already know." Gadget stood firm.

"I didn't think you hated me that much," Stretch said, trying to hide his shock and disappointment.

"I don't hate you. You're one of my best friends. It's just that when it comes to public office, I feel Jack is better qualified."

"How?" Stretch fired back.

"He'd take the job more seriously. I'm tired of seeing

elections like this turn into popularity contests," Gadget said.

"And you think I wouldn't take being president seriously?"

J.R. put his hands together to form a *T*. "Time out, guys, time out. Nobody say another word."

"No way," Chris interrupted, mad now. "Maybe it's time to start talking." He glared at Gadget. "I realize you think you're God's greatest gift to the world of the brainy, but smarts aren't everything."

"And neither is sports," Jack added.

"I never said it was."

"No, you just act like it since your dad was a pro football player."

"Well, it's better than trying to act tough and hide the fact that you're smart, just so people won't tease you," Chris argued back.

"I mean it," J.R. hollered above his friends' loud voices. "Everybody shut up before it's too late."

"It's already too late, J.R.," Chris grumbled. "Come on, Stretch, let's get ready to win the raffle."

"Well, it's the *only* thing you're going to win," Jack shouted after them.

J.R. flung his arms up in the air. "Great, now you've done it," he shouted to his brother.

"Me," Jack snapped back. "I didn't do a thing. Whose side are you on, anyway?"

"The High-Fives," J.R. shouted back, before speaking in a whisper. "But I think I'm the only one."

Chris and Stretch walked away. "I can't believe that guy." Chris was fuming.

"He's got some nerve," Stretch added.

"Yeah, every time we do a sports thing together, we always have to teach Gadget, or keep Jack from blowing his temper. And this is the thanks we get. Well, I'm not trying anymore. As far as I'm concerned, I'll never talk to those guys again." Chris finally sputtered to a stop.

"May I have your attention, please," Max said through an old megaphone. "Sorry to keep you all waiting, but I wanted to give everyone a chance to win." He was a funny-looking man in his midforties with thin, straight greasy hair that he had tried to mold into a helmet to look like Elvis Presley's hair in a picture that hung by the cash register. "It's been a great week and I want to wish everyone good luck. The first item to be won is a 1986 opening day commemorative Mets baseball cap." He put his hand into a large bin filled with cash register receipts. "And the winner is number six-forty-two."

Stretch stared at his copies, checking the numbers. Before he had a chance to finish, a girl standing near some vintage shoes squealed, "I won." The group applauded as she made her way to the front to claim her prize.

"What a waste," Chris grumbled. "She can never know what a great thing she's got."

"Next we have the latest Topps five-pack," Max said

before going through the same motions. The winner was a kid at Bressler Elementary, someone in J.R.'s class.

"Holding out for the good stuff?" J.R. said, joining Stretch and Chris.

"Yeah, I hope so," Stretch said halfheartedly.

"Shouldn't you be with your brother?" Chris said, still angry.

"I told you, I'm not taking sides. And forget everything those guys said. They're just feeling a lot of pressure."

"Right." Chris glared over at them.

"Please don't let this hurt the High-Fives," J.R. pleaded.

"Too late, kid," Chris mumbled. "The High-Fives might be history."

"No!" J.R. shouted.

The audience laughed and stared at J.R. "We've still got a lot of other prizes to give away," Max said with a chuckle. "I realize the Brooks Robinson is a great card, but maybe you'll win the Willie Mays."

"Cool it," Stretch said to J.R. "You just made me miss the number of the winner of the Robinson."

"Sorry," J.R. mumbled. "I thought the High-Fives were more important." He walked away, leaving the two to check the numbers of the next prize.

"That's the third number he's called," Stretch groaned.

"Yeah, those losers are going to be sorry they didn't show up today."

Finally the winner of the baseball card notebook was

there, and Max went on to draw for the Willie Mays. "And the winning number is eight-seventy-five."

"All right!" A shout from across the room drew all the attention.

"Drat," Stretch said, frustrated. "It's Porter."

"Oh, what a waste," Chris grumbled.

"We'll never hear the end of this," Stretch added.

Ron walked to the front of the store and picked up the card. "Eat your hearts out," he said. "And as a reminder to all you seventh graders at Dugan, stick with a winner and vote for me next Friday."

"Oh, brother," Chris groaned.

"And now for the last drawing of the day," Max announced. "The Hank Aaron."

Stretch crossed his fingers and held his breath. Now more than ever he wanted this card. Not just because it was a great card, but because he had to show up Porter. If Stretch didn't win the Aaron, Hank might be tempted to trade Ron's Mays for the Mantle.

"And the winner of the Hank Aaron is number twelve," Max called.

Stretch frantically flipped through his stack. No number twelve. He scanned the room to see who was the lucky winner, but all was silent.

"Okay, let's try another number." Max put his hand in again and this time called out, "Number five-twenty-five."

Stretch could hardly believe it—it was the top receipt on his pile. He darted up to Max and practically grabbed the card from his hands. He held it up in the air. "Now this is a winner," he cried. "And a reminder to vote for a real winner, me, next Friday."

The crowd applauded, and Stretch was mobbed by a group of kids wanting to get a better look at the great card. Among them was Hank Thompson.

"You still up for the trade?" Hank asked.

"I think so," Stretch said, clutching his prize. "I hate to get rid of this, but I've wanted that Mantle for a very long time.

"It's a deal. When do you want to trade?"

"How about right now?" Stretch said with a gulp. He didn't want Porter or anyone else changing Hank's mind.

"Okay, it's right here," Hank said, putting his hand into his pocket. Suddenly a look of panic rushed over his face. "It's gone," he cried. "My 1958 Mickey Mantle is gone."

Everyone took a step back and looked on the floor. "I had it a minute ago, I'm sure it was here," Hank rambled on. "I couldn't have lost it. It's been stolen. My Mickey Mantle has been stolen."

Chapter 13

TO CATCH A THIEF

"This has been a terrible week," Stretch grumbled as he and Chris walked down the empty halls of Dugan Junior High.

"Yeah, and it's only Thursday," Chris replied. "Actually it hasn't been that bad."

"You've got to be joking."

"Well, if you don't count the fact that the '58 Mantle is still missing, or that someone's been writing 'thief' all over your campaign posters."

"Or that half the kids have crossed their names off the big support banner," Stretch added.

"And that we're not talking to half the High-Fives. If you don't count any of those things, it's been a great week."

"Hey, you forgot we have a scrimmage today, and that we're playing the Raiders, or should I say the Condors, Friday night in the city league game."

"Oh, don't remind me. It can't get any worse." Chris stopped Stretch by reaching out and taking his arm. "If you gave the Mantle back, I think it would solve half our problems."

"What?" Stretch shouted, pulling away. "You don't believe what everyone's saying, do you?"

Chris lowered his head. "You're the only one who had a motive for taking it. Everyone knows you've been trying to trade with Hank since the beginning of the season."

"All the more reason for me not to take it, don't you think?" Stretch fired back.

Chris was sympathetic. "I just know how hard it is when someone wants something really bad."

"Like when you wanted to be captain of the soccer team, and stole that stuff from your dad's store?" Stretch said, gently jogging his friend's memory.

Chris's voice grew soft. "I do remember what it's like to be crazed."

"Well, I'm not crazed and I'm not stupid. I didn't take that card," Stretch said simply.

"I believe you, really I do." Chris met his friend's eyes. "But if it doesn't show up soon, you're going to lose the election."

Stretch snapped his fingers and slapped his thighs. "Then we have to find it. We'll search everywhere, everything, and even everyone, until we find it. I've got to clear my name. I want this election more than anything. More than the card, more than the city championship—"

103

"Whoa," Chris said, surprised. "You do want it bad."

Stretch kicked at the floor. "What hurts the most is that the High-Fives are splitting up because of all of this. I'm not sure anything is worth that."

"Yeah, I know. I feel bad about the things I said to Gadget and Jack. I guess I've taken this campaign manager thing too seriously. It's just that they made me so mad."

"I know. They made me mad, too. Maybe after Friday everything will get back to normal, like J.R. said. Well, I'm not ready to give my concession speech yet," Stretch said. "Are you still with me?"

"All the way," Chris stated proudly. "Let's get over to practice, and keep our eyes peeled for that card, or any sign of the thief. We're going to need solid evidence to catch this thief."

Stretch pushed open the double doors that led outside. They both flipped on their baseball caps and jogged to their bikes. It was a quick but quiet ride to the field.

"Hey, what's going on over there?" Chris asked as they stopped and locked their bikes to the metal rack on the far side of the bleachers.

"I don't know, but it looks like a good-size crowd."

"Maybe the Mantle has shown up," Chris said optimistically.

Stretch snap-popped his fingers. "That would be the best thing to happen in a long time."

"Well, let's not wait here. Let's get over there and solve this crime."

"What's up?" Chris asked Alex when they reached the back of the crowd.

"Ah, just some campaign stuff for Jack," she said.

"What is it?" Stretch questioned.

"I think Gadget is using his video camera to make some kind of a music video for Jack's speech." Alex stood on her tiptoes to look over the crowd. "He asked lots of kids to be in it. Seems like it's fun."

"How can you say that? Jack's your competition," Chris stated.

"He's also my friend," Alex added before taking off for the bleachers to watch.

Stretch and Chris inched closer. "Hey, isn't that Eric and Jason?"

"Yeah, what are they doing in Jack's video?" Stretch wondered. "They were just at our poster party."

"Traitors," Chris grumbled. "They were two of our biggest supporters."

"Well, I don't want them if they think I'm a thief," Stretch continued. "Let's go down to the field and warm up with the rest of the team."

They walked through the crowd, but stopped dead in their tracks when they spotted Gadget. On the bleachers was a group of kids dancing on the risers. Gadget's video camera was set up below. Leading the rap song was Gadget. He was dressed in black leather with his hair spiked and an earring dangling from his left lobe.

He held a microphone, and two other guys flanked him, doing rap song sound effects.

> It's Jack with a bat, being where it's at.
> Swinging high, swinging low, making the ball go
> to the left to the right, making a sky flight.
> It's a home run hit, by our main man Klipp.
> Vote for Jack, *clap,* be where it's at,
> I said, vote for Jack, *clap,* be where it's at.
> Yeah, Jack, Jack, v-vote for Jack.

"I can't believe this," Chris said.

"Who'd have believed he had it in him," Stretch added.

"Come on, we've got to keep moving or they'll think we're interested."

"We are interested," Stretch admitted.

"Well, pretend we aren't." The boys sidestepped past the action practically unnoticed, and Stretch set his backpack down on the dugout bench. He heard Gadget holler "Cut" before continuing on with the next shot. As Stretch took his mitt and shoes out, the crowd seemed to be moving toward him.

"Jack is an outstanding sportsman," Gadget said, from behind the camera now. He panned across the field and the crowd and then followed Jack as he stepped into the dugout and sat next to Stretch. Jack started signing autographs for a few kids who'd been sent in to him. "With successful seasons of soccer, basketball, baseball, football, and downhill skiing under his belt, this all-around athlete knows what it takes to be a leader *on* the field and *off.*''

Stretch tried to stay as inconspicuous as possible. He didn't exactly want to be in his opponent's campaign video. He unzipped the small pocket of his backpack and picked up his stack of baseball cards when the camera turned on him.

"Here's one of Jack's teammates," Gadget said proudly. "Don't you agree that Jack is a real asset to the team?"

Stretch set down his cards and glared into the camera lens. "Well, I think you've got the first part of the word right," he said. The crowd laughed and Gadget called "Cut."

He lowered the camera. "Thanks a lot, Evans."

"What did you expect me to say?"

"Actually I should have known better than to expect anything." Gadget shut off the camera and walked away.

The scrimmage that day was disastrous. Without the High-Fives working together, the Lions weren't a team. Instead of calling for catches, Jack and Stretch ran for every hit in the outfield. Twice they crashed into each other, trying not to be outdone. When they did call for a catch, they'd both shout, "I got it." The ball would usually drop between them and the runner would be on his way home.

Gadget at second overthrew a toss to Chris on first so far that Chris would have had to have been ten feet tall to make the play. Chris ran into the batting cage and fell in a heap. The fans snickered. It affected everyone. Even Alex started throwing wild pitches. She and J.R. had their worst day ever, and the Lions lost the scrimmage six to four.

"We had no team play out there today," Coach Holton lectured after the game. "Why didn't you bunt, Jack? Stretch was on first and nobody was out. I know you want to hit a home run, but the situation called for you to get Stretch onto second base. You should have sacrificed your at bat, and done the right thing. Bunt."

"Sorry, Coach," Jack said quietly.

"Stretch, you weren't any better. When Gadget was on second and no one was out, you should have hit a grounder behind him to right field. I've seen you do it a hundred times in practice. You know how important it is to get that runner to third base. Sure you give up the out, but the score was tied at that point and with an error or a wild pitch we would have scored and started a real team rally."

"You're right, Coach," Stretch said, his head low.

"I don't know what effect this election is having anywhere else, but I'll tell you, I hope you guys can get it together soon, 'cause if I were your teammates, I wouldn't vote at all. You've got two days before the game with the Condors. If you recall, our scrimmage with them was not a good sign of what you can do. They are the toughest team to beat, so let's get our priorities straight and play some ball."

The boys exchanged glances, but were too embarrassed to say anything. A lot had happened, Stretch thought, and as much as he wanted to change things, he wasn't prepared to make the first move. He nudged Chris. "Come on, let's get out of here."

"Right," Chris whispered back.

"Why don't you come over for dinner and we can talk about what we want to do about the rest of this campaign." The boys walked across the field and turned back to see J.R. walking alone and Jack and Gadget heading for Gadget's house. They hadn't been to Mike's together for over a week.

"Who can that be?" Stretch said, glancing up at the clock in the Evanses' kitchen after the doorbell rang.

"It's nine o'clock," Carol Evans, Stretch's mom, said. She peered out the living room window, Stretch and Chris right behind her. She flicked on the front step light. "It's Gadget, Jack, and J.R."

Chris and Stretch shared a surprised look. "Let them in," Stretch stated.

Mrs. Evans opened the door. "Come on in, boys. What brings you out so late on a school night?"

"We have to talk to Stretch," Gadget said.

"It's a matter of life and death," J.R. said dramatically.

Jack elbowed his brother. "It's very important, and we're sorry it's so late."

"Come on in," Mrs. Evans said again. "I've missed not having you boys around. Come into the kitchen. I think there are just enough brownies to go around."

"Actually we need to use your VCR," Gadget said.

Chris went on the defensive. "Look, if you think we're going to help you with your campaign, you're crazy."

"I knew they'd react like this," Jack snapped. "They don't even realize that we're trying to save their campaign."

"Save it?" Stretch asked.

"Trust me," Gadget said, walking down the stairs to the basement. "After you see this video, you'll know what we mean." He went straight into the recreation room. He took the tape out of its jacket and slipped it into the VCR slot. After pushing a few buttons, and adjusting the tracking, a picture of Gadget doing the rap song came up on the screen.

"We saw all of this today, Gadget," Chris said. "We were there, remember?"

"Just relax, Morton," Jack replied. "Now keep your eyes open. I think you'll be surprised."

The rap ended and the autograph and interview scene came into view. "We were trying to edit out the part where you were on camera, and we found something very interesting," Gadget said.

"Watch very closely," J.R. added.

Stretch and Chris strained to watch, but didn't notice anything out of the ordinary.

"And freeze," Gadget shouted. He stopped at a frame where Stretch had opened up the small pocket of his backpack, revealing his trading cards. "Check out the top card."

"It's the Hank Aaron," Stretch said. "Big deal. Everybody knows I've got that card. Even you guys saw me win it."

"Okay," Gadget continued. "Obviously we couldn't use the rest of this interview, so we were going to edit it out."

"But we thought you should see something first," J.R. said. "See, when Gadget yells 'Cut,' he lowers the camera, but he doesn't turn it off. The camera is taking a picture of the bench."

"Or, more accurately," Gadget interrupted, "your backpack and cards."

"Watch closely," Jack added.

In the next few frames the boys listened to the argument between Gadget and Stretch, but in the background they saw something more revealing. Crouched behind the bench in the crowd of kids was Ron Porter. He took something out of his pocket and slipped it on top of Stretch's card pile. "Freeze," Gadget said again, pausing the frame. "It's a little fuzzy, but you can see it," he said proudly.

The screen was a jumble of white and black static, but there was no mistake about what had happened. "It's the Mantle," Stretch shouted as he pressed his nose practically onto the screen. "That's proof I didn't steal it."

"Precisely," Gadget answered. "Porter's planted it on you, though. Luckily we have the evidence that you didn't take it."

Chris stood up slowly. "I can't believe it."

"Why would he do a thing like that?" Stretch muttered.

"Do you think Hank was in on it?" Chris asked.

"Those dirty rats," Stretch said, slamming a fist into his other palm.

Gadget turned off the machine. "We're not sure who's in on it, but you can bet that Porter was going to have you caught red-handed at school tomorrow. It would totally ruin any chance of yours to win the election."

"You guys could have gone along with it," Chris said quietly to Gadget and Jack.

"Believe me," Jack said, "I thought about it."

"For about two seconds," J.R. added.

"As mad as I am at you guys, it's still not right. Besides, if I went along with Porter, it would make me as bad as he is."

"I don't know what to say," Stretch said, embarrassed.

"Look, we've all said a lot of bad stuff this week," J.R. continued. "I think we owe each other an apology. And after that's done, I think we'd better come up with a plan to clear Stretch's name and get Porter in the hot seat for a change. What do you say?"

"I say I've been a jerk," Stretch said, holding up his hand for Jack to high-five. "Forgive me?"

"Done," Jack answered, slapping back. "Forgive me?"

"That goes for me, too," Gadget added.

"Count me in double," Chris topped.

"That seals it," J.R. said, adding the last high-five. "All for one, and one for all. Let's get to work."

Chapter 14

THE VOTE THAT COUNTS

"That was a stroke of genius, suggesting ladies first," Stretch said to Jack the next day before the final campaign speeches. "With Alex going first, and Porter second, we'll be able to expose him before our speeches."

"Good luck," Jack said to Stretch.

"You, too," Stretch answered. "It doesn't seem as important as it did a week ago, huh?"

"Not really. It's been a pretty lousy week."

"That's for sure," Stretch said with a smile. "Can I help you with the VCR or the screen?"

"It's all set and ready to go," Jack replied. "Gadget's a whiz at that stuff."

"Is Chris ready, too?" Stretch asked.

Jack sighed. "I hope so, because if they don't follow through, we're in big trouble."

"With egg on our faces," Stretch added.

A loud noise came from the other side of the curtain. "Hey, I think the kids are starting to file in. See you out front."

"Man, I don't know what I'm more nervous about, the plan or the speech." Stretch high-fived Jack's hands. "I'll say one thing, though, it sure is nice to be working together again." They took their places in front of the curtain on the Dugan Junior High auditorium stage.

Stretch watched the students slowly file in. The day had finally arrived. The day he'd dreamed about for the last ten days. He didn't feel the same about the election anymore. He wasn't even sure he wanted to win, or maybe he wasn't sure he deserved to win. Stretch smiled as he remembered the night before when all the High-Fives were finally reunited in his basement. It was the biggest high, bigger than any school election could ever be. It was like a grand slam home run, a real vote of confidence from his friends. Once again the High-Fives had stuck together. Now they had the most important thing to finish, and Stretch took a deep breath and hoped they'd be successful.

Mr. Mills introduced the seventh grade nominees for the last time. Stretch could tell by the applause that Porter's scheme was working. Finally it was time for the candidates' speeches, and Alex was at the podium ready to deliver hers. Cathy Sullivan had been her campaign manager. There hadn't been that many posters around school for her, but he'd seen Alex's neon-colored stickers and buttons on a lot of the kids, especially the girls. She'd make a good president, Stretch thought. She finished her speech and there was solid applause and response from the class. Now it was Porter's turn.

"Here we go," Chris whispered to Gadget from their seats on the opposite side of the podium from Stretch and Jack.

"As long as there isn't a blackout we should be able to make our point," Gadget said.

"Our next seventh grade presidential candidate is Ron Porter," Mr. Mills, the student council adviser, said, introducing Ron. Ron walked confidently to the podium as Greg, his campaign manager, manned the overhead projector.

"A president should be a man you can trust," Ron began. "Someone you look up to and trust." Greg slid a picture of Abe Lincoln into the projector. "A man who is strong." Rambo's picture went in next. "A man with brains." Albert Einstein's picture filled the screen. "An honest man who won't try to trick you, or lead you the wrong way."

Before Greg could put up the next selection, Chris yanked out the cord and Gadget plugged in the VCR. The section of tape where Porter was planting the Mantle in Stretch's bag rose ten feet high in front of the whole school. Gadget had copied it six times so it kept repeating the act again and again.

"What's going on?" Ron shouted from the podium.

"Turn that thing off," Greg shouted, too.

"Look up there," Chris said, pointing to the screen. "What's Ron doing?"

"It's the missing Mickey Mantle card," Gadget said right on cue.

"He's putting the card in Stretch's pack," Jack shouted.

"Pull the cord," Ron demanded when he turned around and saw himself framing Stretch.

Greg yanked the cord off the overhead projector but nothing happened. It just hung loose in his hand. "It's not working," he shouted back to Ron.

"Stretch didn't steal anything," Chris said.

"It was honest Ron," Gadget said sarcastically.

"I was framed," Stretch said, standing on his chair.

"Porter's the real crook," Jack added.

Ron ran in front of the screen and held his arms in front of the image. "I am not a crook," he repeated over and over.

Randy jumped up from the vice-presidential seats and turned on the auditorium lights. Gadget turned off the VCR, but when Greg hooked up the overhead again, the Mickey Mantle was being projected ten feet high on the screen.

"That was a close one," Chris said, sliding back into his seat. "I thought we weren't going to get a chance to put it back."

Gadget smiled. "Great work."

"Order, let's have order," Mr. Mills called into the

microphone. He snatched the baseball card off the overhead. "Who does this belong to?"

The High-Fives all pointed to Hank Thompson, and Mr. Mills motioned for him to come up on stage and pick it up. Nervously he stumbled up the stairs and stood in front of the microphone.

"Ron made me give it to him. All I wanted to do was trade it for the Hank Aaron. It wasn't supposed to be like this," Hank said, choking.

Stretch felt sorry for him, because it wasn't the first time Porter had pushed him around. "Poor kid," he mumbled.

Mr. Mills took the stand again. "I think if everyone is ready to settle down we can continue. Ron, would you like to finish your presentation?"

Ron started to stand, but most of the students booed him. Even Stretch felt a little sorry for him, too. Ron sat down and shook his head, staring at the floor.

"We'll move to our next candidate then," Mr. Mills said, and Jack stepped up in front of the class.

"Fellow students, candidates, and faculty," Jack began. "I'd like to thank you for this honor."

For the first time Stretch really looked at Jack as a candidate. Instead of seeing the tough kid who always had a chip on his shoulder, he saw an intelligent, hardworking guy who'd had a life that was tougher than his. Stretch found himself thinking about how lucky he'd been to have things easy. How nice it was to be good at baseball, or to be able to rely on his sense of humor in a difficult situation. He admired Jack, and decided if nothing else came of the election, he had learned to look at people more closely, even when the person was one of your closest friends. Suddenly it was his turn to speak, and Stretch felt awkward and afraid.

He set down the index cards with his prepared speech written on them. He stared at the students and cleared his throat. "Most of you seventh graders know me as the class clown or as the baseball player. It's true, that's a lot of what I'm about, but there's also a part of me that isn't funny or isn't into playing a game. I guess that's why I want to be your president. Like baseball, a class is a team effort. It's the students who make the decisions; the president just puts them into action. I can go to bat for you, maybe even hit a grand slam, but you have to be ready to run the bases. I can tell you *how* to steal a base, but you'll have to do it yourself when the opportunity's right. I can encourage you to make that catch, but the glove is on your hand. I guess what I'm trying to say is that there are other candidates who can fill the job of president as well as I can, and they probably want it as much as I do, too. You have to make that decision. I'm ready to take on the responsibility. But no matter if I win today or not, I'm going to give my best for my class. I've learned that sticking together and having friends is the first step to making things happen, and believe me this class is happening. Thank you."

Stretch sat down as the applause built. He hadn't said what he'd planned to say, but he'd said what he felt, and he'd said what he wanted to. Now it was up to the voters.

"You guys were incredible," J.R. said after the rally.

"Hey, dude," Stretch said, giving him a high-five, "how'd you get here?"

"Just 'cause I can't vote doesn't mean I can't be here. Mom wrote me a note so I could get out for your special assembly. The Porter thing went real well, don't you think?"

"It got the job done," Jack said.

"I'm just glad people don't think I'm some kind of rip-off artist," Stretch added.

"Now all we have to do is wait until the last class of the day to find out the results," Gadget said, gathering his equipment together.

"Yeah, may the best man win," Stretch said.

"And don't forget we've got that big game today," Chris added.

"With the Condors," J.R. said with a shudder.

"Oh, man, are they going to be mad," Stretch added.

Gadget pushed his glasses up. "Look, we didn't do anything bad. If Porter hadn't tried to blackball Stretch, he wouldn't have had to face the crowd today."

"Let's not talk about it anymore. It's done and things have been set right. Now we have to go on, okay?" Stretch said.

"Right," J.R. said. "I've got to hustle. If I don't get back before math, it'll be Mrs. Dean's spelling lists for me."

"Oh, man, I forgot about her," Jack teased.

"She's still there."

"See you at the park," Stretch called after him. "If you want to try some special practice swings, get there early."

"Great," J.R. answered. "Something tells me I'm going to need it today."

Stretch was surprised at how relaxed he was the rest of the day. He felt like a big weight had been lifted from him, and, of course, it had. All day kids' signatures started reappearing on the banner, and lots of kids came up to tell him that they'd voted for him. Stretch was proud.

"So, you ready?" Chris asked as the two buddies were about to enter their homeroom class.

"Ready as I'll ever be," Stretch answered. He walked confidently into the room and calmly sat at his desk.

"No matter what happens now," Greg Forbes said, "you'd better be prepared to play your best game ever today. The Condors are out to cream you guys."

Stretch just smiled. "I'll be there."

The box in the corner clicked on with static, and Mrs. Sandy wished Stretch and Kaitlyn good luck.

"Thanks for all your help," Stretch said to Chris.

"My pleasure. I just hope my pushiness didn't wreck it for you."

"No way, man," Stretch answered back. Once again Stretch was numb as the winners for secretary, treasurer, and vice-president were announced. Kaitlyn had won the secretary spot, and Stretch wondered if he'd feel as good as she did in the next few minutes. Randy Salazar had lost, and Stretch took that as a good omen as far as Porter was concerned. Right then he hoped he'd be a good loser or a good winner. He felt like a winner, and that's what really mattered.

"And the new seventh grade president is"—Mr. Mills announced—"Alex Tye."

Stretch smiled and looked at Chris. "She'll do a good job."

"Let's give our new officers all the support we can," Mrs. Sandy said. "As Stretch said in his speech this morning, we all have to run the bases."

Stretch felt great, and he felt even better when his homeroom class voted him their student council representative. He'd made that grand slam after all.

About the Author

S. S. GORMAN grew up in Greeley, Colorado, with two older brothers and two younger brothers. The family was always active in sports. Their favorites include skiing, skating, softball, golf, tennis, swimming, hiking, fishing, basketball, and football. Ms. Gorman has a B.S. degree from Colorado State University and an M.A. from the University of Northern Colorado. For the past fifteen years she has worked as a professional performer onstage and in radio and film, as well as writing several young-adult novels. The titles in *The High-Fives* series are: *Soccer Is a Kick, Slam Dunk, Home Run Stretch, Quarterback Sneak, Skiing for the Prize,* and *Grand Slam,* available from Minstrel Books. She currently lives in California with her husband and two children.